I BO⌷  S

Series Boxed Set

TONYA BROOKS

First Edition Copyright © 2017 by Tonya Brooks
Book Cover by Envy Designs

AUTHORS NOTE

The I Boinked The Boss Series is a collection of short stories that have one common theme, *getting down and dirty with the boss!*

ACKNOWLEDGEMENTS:

To my wonderful Beta Team: Susan, Greta, Karina, Lorrie, Frankie, Karen, Pam, Amanda and Michal.
Y'all freaking rock!

To the members of Tonya's Tribe for all of your love and support!

And my wonderful husband, Billy. Thank you for your unwavering encouragement, your never ending patience with my writing obsession, and most of all, for loving me. You are my beloved, my rock, my inspiration, my everything!

Table of Contents

TONYA BROOKS

SHE'S UNDER MY
Skin

I BOINKED THE BOSS SERIES

SHE'S UNDER MY SKIN
I Boinked The Boss Series

TONYA BROOKS

CHAPTER ONE

Chase Marlowe came awake slowly, the heavy metal drum solo resonating in his head felt like he'd tied one on last night. Damn Saige for ordering wine with dinner. She knew it left him feeling like shit the next day. Groaning in pain, he rolled gingerly onto his back, raising his left arm over his eyes to block the light.

His right hand slid down his abdomen, and oddly enough, he was not greeted by his usual morning wood. Huh. Maybe he *had* tied one on. Eyes open mere slits, he slid gingerly off the bed and staggered into the bathroom. Without turning on the light, he managed to locate the toilet, lifted the lid and pissed himself.

What. The. Fuck?

Yep, no doubt about it. Hot urine had run down his leg to puddle under his foot. Muttering foul imprecations, he stepped away from the toilet, snatched a towel off of the rod and scrubbed his leg. Dropping the towel on the floor, he used his foot to swipe it at the puddle and reached for his misbehaving dick.

His hand encountered neatly trimmed pubic hair, but no dick. Both hands joined the search and his brain cleared instantly when he realized it wasn't there. His dick was gone. Holy hell! *His dick was gone!* Flipping the light on, he bent over and stared in alarm at... *a vagina?* Mother of God. *His dick was gone... and he had a vagina!?!*

Chase staggered backward as he stood upright, grabbing his chest because his damn heart had stopped. But that wasn't *his* chest he grabbed. It felt like... his eyes nearly bugged out of his head as he looked down and saw breasts. *Why the hell did he have breasts? And a vagina?*

AND WHERE THE FUCK WAS HIS DICK!?!

Whirling to face the mirror in complete and utter shock, he saw the hottest *female* body he'd ever laid eyes on reflected back at him. Lifting his astonished gaze to meet the sage green eyes of his reflection, he damn near had a heart attack on the spot. He was staring at a *woman*!

But not just any woman.

No, the woman in the mirror was his man-hungry, hotter than hell, set your balls on fire with a look, personal assistant. The woman who tormented and teased him on a daily basis. The woman he wanted more than the air he breathed. The woman with the body he'd wished countless times that he could have.

Huh. Looked like he'd gotten his wish.

Holy fucking hell!

He all but ran through the suite to get to her room, flung the door open and nearly passed out cold when he saw *himself* sprawled across the king size bed. His wild-eyed gaze homed in on his missing dick and the hand that held it. It was Saige. He knew it. *And she was holding his dick!* "Don't touch my dick!"

***

Saige DeLancey bolted upright in bed and stared at... *herself?* She blinked, shook her head and blinked again. Yep, it was her all right. Standing in the doorway bare ass naked. Wow. Those grueling mornings at the gym were really paying off. Her thighs were looking really toned and... wait, *what?*

Holy hell. *She was hallucinating.*

Wait. *Why* was she hallucinating? And if she was gonna hallucinate about someone standing in her hotel room bare ass naked, why couldn't it have been Chase? Lord, what she wouldn't give to see him in the buff. The man was built like a Greek god. Mmm, she'd bet he had a nice package to go with that muscular body.

The other her glared at her and stalked over to the bed to grab her hand and growl, "Don't handle the goods."

Saige looked at herself as if she had gone insane, and the thought *did* occur to her that she might be mentally unbalanced. Then she looked down at her hand that the hallucination was holding onto. Her very *masculine* hand that was connected to a muscular forearm covered in dark brown hair. She closed her eyes and muttered, "Yep. I'm batshit crazy."

"Look in the mirror, Saige," her voice commanded as the sheet was pulled up over her lower half.

"Nope. I'm good," she refused and threw her other hand over her eyes to block out the illusion. "Great. Now I'm talking to myself."

"Oh, it gets worse," her voice warned and pulled her hand away from her eyes. "Look in the mirror."

Saige opened her eyes, looked over at the mirror mounted above the dresser and saw Chase sitting in the bed. *Holy Hannah...* his body was glorious! Broad shoulders, big, strong arms, well-defined chest and holy shit, was that an *eight-pack* of abs? The man looked lickable. God, she'd love to lick every last inch and...

Wait. Why was she staring at *Chase* in the mirror instead of herself? Because the reflection showed her standing beside the bed, not sitting on it. *Holy Mother of God!* She sprang out of the bed and watched incredulously as Chase's image did the same thing.

Whoa, mama, she'd been right about his package. The man was hung like a... *What. The. Fuck?* His image did everything she did. Her jaw dropped and so did his. Saige grasped her face with both hands and so did he. Her knees went weak and she sank down on the edge of the bed in shock. *And so did he.*

Looking up at the other her in astonishment, she saw herself nod in confirmation. "What the hell is going on?" She demanded.

"I'm you and you're me," he responded grimly.

"Seriously?" If ever a look said, *Duh*, his did. She got up and began to pace back and forth in agitation, her brain working feverishly to try and come up with a rational explanation as to why she was having an out of body experience. The logical reason would be... "Oh my God! We're dead, aren't we?"

He snorted at that. "Don't be ridiculous, Saige," Chase chastened as he reached out and poked her arm with a finger. "We're still corporeal. Just in the wrong bodies."

"How does something like this happen?" She demanded, at a complete loss.

"How the hell should I know?" He complained and his perplexed expression assured her that he was just as baffled as she felt.

***

"You're the genius," she accused as if that meant he should know everything.

"This," he said and gestured a hand between the two of them. "Defies the laws of science. It's *not* possible."

She reached down, grabbed his favorite appendage and demanded, "Then explain why I have a dick."

Chase snatched her hand away. "Rule number one: don't touch my dick. For any reason," he insisted.

"Are you kidding me?" Saige countered in disbelief. "We've been *body snatched* and you're making up rules?"

Damn right he was. Rules meant things were well ordered and since just being near her always left his mind in a state of chaos, and his body aching with desire, they were also mandatory. "Rule number two: don't look at it either."

Giving him the evil eye, she admitted, "Your ass itches. Can I scratch it or is there a rule about that, too?"

"Goddammit, Saige, will you be serious?" Chase complained and raked a hand through his hair, only to have his fingers get tangled in the long curly tresses. "We've got to have some ground rules until we get this situation resolved."

"Fine," she snapped and walked around him. "Make your silly rules."

"Where the hell are you going?"

"I have to pee."

Which meant she'd have to touch his dick. Shit. This could get complicated. "I'll help."

That announcement stopped her in her tracks and Saige turned around to stare at him in disbelief. *"Excuse me?"*

"I said I'll help."

"Help me *pee*?"

"It isn't as easy as you think," he assured her, recalling the fiasco he'd had.

***

"Not happening," Saige denied as she walked into the en suite and was shocked when he walked in right behind her. "Chase, get the hell out."

"Not happening," he parroted.

She placed her hand against his chest to stop his progress, absently noticing that her breasts felt nice and firm, *thank God*. "I'm a grown woman. I don't need help."

"Yeah? When was the last time you peed while holding a dick?" He asked sarcastically and her scowl became a wicked smile. "Never mind. I don't want to know."

"I appreciate the concern, but I've got this," she said confidently as she gave his chest a little shove and had to grab his shoulders when he almost fell backward. Well, hell. Chase obviously had the strength to go along with those yummy muscles.

"You are not handling my junk," he insisted adamantly and quickly scooted around her.

"Fine. Stay, but you're *not* helping," she snapped as she walked over to the toilet and plopped her butt down on it. That maneuver would have proved effective if his dick had been limp. Since it wasn't, she sighed in vexation and scowled down at the very well endowed specimen standing at full attention.

"That's not going to work," he pointed out as he clapped a hand over her eyes. "Stop looking, dammit."

"Make it go away," she insisted and wished that he could make this whole nightmare go away.

"Close your eyes and stand up."

"No."

"Jesus Christ. Stop being so damn difficult."

Sighing in exasperation, she batted his hand away and glared at him as she stood. Once her eyes were closed, Chase turned her to face the toilet, reached around her and firmly grasped his... oh, God, *her* dick, angling it downward. And wasn't that the weirdest damn sensation that she'd ever experienced. Although the dick seemed to enjoy it.

"Pee."

"I don't think I can now," she admitted, too engrossed in those heretofore never experienced sensations to concentrate on anything else. His hand felt cool and soft against her engorged flesh, his grip firm but gentle. She flexed her hips instinctively and drew in a ragged breath when the dick pumped in and out of that not quite tight enough fist, the slide of flesh on flesh sending her pulse racing.

***

"Stop that!" Chase ordered and tightened his grip on his dick, pressing his body in tight against the back side of hers to prevent further movement. Jesus H. Christ! The last thing he needed was Saige feeling him get his rocks off.

"You liked it," she accused.

Damn right he liked it. He was a man after all. Or at least *he had been* the night before. No way in hell did he want her knowing anything about his sexual likes or dislikes. He had a hard enough time keeping her at a distance like it was. "Just pee," he commanded and hoped like hell the woman actually listened for a change.

***

She did. Only because her bladder was really beginning to protest. Saige concentrated on peeing and urine shot out of the end of the dick with startling force, causing the water in the toilet to splash. She squealed in surprise and stopped the flow while Chase muttered imprecations behind her.

After two more attempts, she finally got it to flow at a steady pace. Saige realized that peeing as a man might be more convenient because they could stand, but it was a lot more complicated than peeing as a woman. When Chase shook the now semi-erect appendage, she burst into unrestrained laughter.

"Whatever you're thinking, *don't* say it," he warned and reached around her to flush the toilet.

"I'm thinking that I've either lost my mind or this is the most bizarre dream I've ever had," she admitted as she turned around and looked down at his scowling face. "Tell me we're stoned."

"We're screwed," he admitted as he washed his hands.

"Maybe we should *get* stoned."

He grabbed the bathrobe from the back of the door and slipped it on her. Pulling the sides together, he pulled the sash tight and tied it in a double knot. Now that she was covered, he felt a small measure of control in what had become an out of control situation. "What we need is coffee," he said reasonably as he exited the room.

"Wait. Why is it that I'm not even allowed to look at your body and you're parading around naked in mine?" Saige demanded as she followed him.

"I won't be in a minute," he denied as he crossed the lounge area and headed into the other bedroom to grab the hotel robe. He pulled it on and had to push the sleeves up when they hung past his fingertips. Damn. He'd never really realized just how tiny she was until then. The robe swallowed her whole.

"My robe will fit better," she offered as she held up a slinky scrap of silk that lay across the foot of the bed.

Yeah, but Chase was certain that it would reveal a hell of a lot more than he needed to see, too. The image of her fine assed body was permanently burned into his retinas like it was. Damn total recall. "This is fine."

Saige tossed the robe back on the bed and asked, "So how do we figure out how we wound up in each other's bodies?"

"I'm more concerned about how to switch back," he replied as he ushered her back into the lounge. When a knock sounded at the door, he asked impatiently, "Now what?"

"Probably room service," she said as she glanced at her watch. "I ordered breakfast for seven because the meeting is at..." Saige broke off with a gasp and they stared at each other in dawning horror.

"Mother fuck," Chase muttered under his breath as he raked both hands through his hair and got all of his fingers tangled in those luxurious blonde curls. There was no way he could appear at the meeting like this. What the hell was he supposed to do now?

***

The knock sounded again and Saige went to answer it. She opened the door and gave the handsome young waiter the once over. "Well, good morning," she purred flirtatiously and saw his expression become horrified.

Remembering that she was a man, she barely restrained herself from laughing because the waiter probably thought that Chase was gay. The limp dick that lay against her thigh assured her that he was not. *Thank God.* "Just put it over there," she suggested with an airy wave of her hand that did nothing to dispel the notion.

Turning to follow the waiter, she noticed Chase standing by the floor to ceiling windows, arms folded across his chest, feet spread wide, scowling at her. That pose was his standard go to when he was trying to look intimidating. This time he looked like a pissed off kitten and she had to bite her lip to stop the laughter from escaping.

***

"Just leave the cart," Chase said curtly as he signed the ticket, adding a generous tip. He was going to wring her neck for this. Once they were alone, he snapped, "You just had to flirt with him, didn't you?"

Lifting the covers off of the plates, she shrugged and replied without an ounce of remorse, "He was cute."

"Dammit, Saige, he thinks I'm gay."

"Would you rather he knew you were a woman?" She shot back in amusement.

"Jesus H. Christ," he growled and raked a hand through his hair, getting his fingers tangled in those goddamn curls again. "Do you take anything seriously?"

"The only thing I want to be serious about right now is coffee," she replied as she sat down at the table and crossed her legs. "Ouch, dammit!"

"What's wrong?"

***

"I now understand why men don't cross their legs," she admitted as the pain from having his junk pinched between her thighs began to subside.

Chase looked appalled. "Easy with the goods," he half warned, half pleaded.

"Speaking of the goods," she said as she poured them both a cup of coffee. "What's up with the paranoia about me getting a peek?"

He sat in the opposite chair and looked at her as if she'd just asked the most ridiculous question he'd ever heard. "Seeing each other naked would make working together awkward," he said seriously.

"You held my dick while I peed," she reminded him. "Doesn't get more awkward than that."

"I just don't think it's a good idea for us to have any physical contact with each other's bodies," he said stubbornly as he reached for the cup and had to shove the sleeve back up his arm and out of the way.

She blinked at him over the cup as if he were dense. "You held my dick. While I peed."

Sighing wearily, he clarified, "Technically, I held *my* dick while *I* peed."

Saige smirked at him. "*Physically*, it's mine and possession is nine-tenths of the law."

"That's *my* dick," he growled and she dissolved into laughter.

"You're so territorial," she grinned wickedly. "Mind you, it's a *very* nice dick..."

"Saige," he warned.

"But I'll happily return it just as soon as you figure out how to get me the hell *out of your body*." Okay, so her voice had gotten a little shrill at the end, but dammit, she was about to have a major freak out and he wasn't helping. Saige used humor to cope with uncomfortable situations and she'd never been in one anywhere near as bad as this.

***

He wished like hell he knew how. Deciding to treat this like any other experiment, Chase said, "Let's go over the facts."

"I have a dick and you don't."

He gave her a quelling look. "Did anything unusual happen yesterday?"

"Like the plane getting lost in the Bermuda Triangle and we wound up in an alternate reality?"

With a long-suffering look, he asked, "Were you exposed to any chemicals in the lab?"

"I didn't even go into the lab yesterday," she denied. "The closest I came to chemicals was the wine we had with din..." Saige's eyes grew round and her mouth dropped open.

"What?" He demanded anxiously.

"Oh my God. Oh my God, oh my God, oh. My. *God!*"

"Saige, what the hell is it?" He demanded, all sorts of horrible possibilities of things she could have come into contact with in his lab flying through his mind.

"The fortune cookie."

"What about it?" He frowned.

"It came true," she breathed in horror.

"Impossible," Chase scoffed.

She fixed him with a look and pointed out, "I have a dick."

And he didn't.

Mother fuck. All right, it was time to turn off the analytical portion of his brain and accept that the impossible had already happened so he could figure out how to reverse it. "What did it say?"

She surged up from the chair and ran over to the coffee table to grab the oversized handbag she persisted in carrying and upended the contents onto the couch. Digging through a mind-boggling array of junk, she found the small slip of paper and read it aloud. *"The third time you make a wish it will come true."*

"What the hell does that mean?"

"I made the same wish three times last night," she confessed and looked mortified. "The first time was when we were walking to the restaurant and saw that falling star. The second time was when we stopped by the fountain on the way back and threw some change in. The third time was when I read the fortune cookie."

Mother of God. Chase realized that *he* had made the same wish three times yesterday as well. When she had insisted they make a wish on a star, at the damn fountain, and while he'd watched her curvaceous little ass walking into her bedroom after dinner. All three times he had wished… *that he could have her gorgeous body.*

His voice was strangled when he asked, "What did you wish for?"

"You were being such a pain in the ass yesterday that I wished…" she closed her eyes as if she were in pain and then met his frown when she admitted, "I wished that we could trade places for a day."

The rational part of his brain scoffed at the very idea of wishes coming true, but the rest of him latched onto one part of her confession like a lifeline. "*A day*? Are you sure it was just a day?" He asked hopefully and saw her nod in confirmation. "Then we just have to get through today and let this thing run its course."

"The meeting is today," she reminded him. "And *you're* the main event."

"We'll cancel."

"Chase, you can't back out of an appointment with the freaking Joint Chiefs of Staff," Saige pointed out. That was the reason why they were in DC. He was meeting with the highest ranking members of the armed forces at the Pentagon to brief them on a new form of body armor that he had developed. "You *have* to do this."

"You mean *you* have to."

"Oh, shit."

Yeah. They were so screwed.

CHAPTER TWO

Chase chugged coffee and racked his brain for a solution to the newest twist in this nightmare. There was no way in hell that she could give the presentation. Saige was not one of his lab assistants. She was his *administrative* assistant and completely clueless about the complexities of his design.

Her area of expertise was keeping him on task and on schedule. Not an easy feat to accomplish at the best of times and practically impossible when a new idea sparked his interest. He could be grumpy, overbearing and a downright tyrant at times, which is probably why she made the damn wish, to begin with.

But Saige knew how to deal with all of his moods and did so with relentless fervor. She employed every tactic from cajoling to blackmail to keep him on track. And she had no qualms about telling him off or putting him in his place when required. The woman was completely indispensable because he'd be lost without her.

In more ways than one.

"How about this," she suggested while pacing a trench in the carpet. "You have a throat injury and can't speak so your assistant has to do all the talking."

He considered the idea, decided it had merit and nodded. "What kind of injury?"

"Hell, I don't know," she complained as if it made little difference. "Laryngitis. Chemical exposure. Oral sex."

"Oral sex?" He repeated absently, his mind filtering through a variety of chemicals that could cause temporary paralysis of the vocal cords without permanent damage.

"It happens," she confirmed. "It's not as easy as it looks to deep throat."

"Dammit, Saige. Can you be serious?" Chase snapped in aggravation when he realized what she was saying.

"Hey, I take blow jobs very seriously," she insisted indignantly. "Men *usually* appreciate that."

He didn't know whether to kiss her or kill her. If he still had a dick, it would have been standing at attention and throbbing painfully. The mental imagery of her luscious lips wrapped around it was enough to make a man insane. Chase should know. He'd been fantasizing about it since the day he'd met her.

Forcing his mind back to the subject at hand, *the absence of said dick*, he replied, "Laryngitis due to chemical fume exposure will work. Just keep your mouth shut and let me do the talking."

"Exactly what I had planned to do while I was in *my* body," she said with a smirk and glanced at the watch on her wrist. "We'd better get ready."

Chase countered with, "We have plenty of time. It only takes me ten minutes."

"When was the last time you put on makeup?" She queried with a smirk.

A scowl covered his face as he admitted, "You don't need all of that crap to look beautiful."

"Right. Like you'd notice if my hair was on fire," she derided.

Oh, he'd notice all right. There wasn't a damn thing about her that he *didn't* notice. Or have committed to memory. *Permanently.* "I don't have the time or the patience for girly nonsense," he said blandly.

"And I refuse to be seen in public looking like a hag," she refused and placed her hands on her hips. "So get your ass in the shower, big boy. It takes thirty minutes just to blow dry my hair."

The shower. *Sonofabitch.* "We'll have to shower together."

Her mouth dropped open in shock. "What?"

"The rules," he explained wearily. "Since there's no looking or touching, I wash you and you wash me."

A wicked smile curved her lips and she asked, "Care to repeat that offer once we're not body snatched?"

God, would he ever.

Unfortunately, their association had to remain professional. She went through men like they were disposable and Chase believed in lasting relationships. If they were intimate, he wouldn't be able to go back to platonic co-workers and Saige would never settle down with one man. It was a no-win situation.

So he did the only thing he could. He kept her close enough, but not too close. Being with her and not being able to act on his feelings was heaven and hell. But it was better than trying to have more and losing what little he did have of her. Yeah. *He was pathetic*. Saige already owned his heart, and if they ever made love, she'd own his soul as well.

"No," he replied bluntly and rose. "Shower time."

* * *

"Jesus, Chase. You're not scrubbing mud off your car," Saige complained a few minutes later as she stood in the shower. He was standing behind her, washing her with brisk efficiency as if she were an inanimate object.

"Sorry," he muttered and his ministrations instantly slowed, becoming almost gentle.

As awkward as the situation was, she wanted to enjoy the feel of his hands on her body. Even if it wasn't *her* body. Especially since it was probably the only time it would ever happen. Damn the man. Chase might be a certified genius, but he was as dense as mud when it came to understanding women.

Or at least he was with her.

Her feelings for him were so obvious that everyone in the lab knew she was crazy about him. But the brilliant scientist remained hopelessly clueless. Saige was certain that the only way she'd ever get his laser-like focus directed at her was if she contracted an incurable disease. Obviously, unrequited love didn't count.

Because she was madly in love with her maddening boss.

Chase was the typical absent-minded professor who forgot to eat unless she put food in front of him. And he was so dedicated to his work that he didn't know what day it was half of the time. He had a tendency to get sidetracked easily and since her job entailed keeping him on task, they butted heads on a daily basis. The lab staff said they argued like an old married couple.

Which they did.

So why did she love the infuriating man?

Because he also had a wicked sense of humor, possessed lethal amounts of charm and behaved like an honest to God gentleman when he wasn't in mad scientist mode. Which wasn't often, but on the rare occasions that he let the man hidden behind the lab coat out to play, it never failed to melt her heart all over again.

The professor might be a pain in her ass, but the man was just too loveable.

Damn him.

Oh, my. That was interesting.

Chase had moved in front of her and began washing her chest. The lower his hand went, the more erect her newly acquired dick became. The breath caught in her throat when the soapy washcloth cupped her balls. Her heart began to hammer as he gently washed the now hard as granite appendage.

Unable to resist, she opened her eyes and looked down. The image was surreal, yet the most erotic thing she'd ever seen. There she knelt, her cloth covered hand wrapped around Chase's dick. *His very large, extremely hard, dick*. The moan of pleasure that escaped her lips sounded more like a groan.

"Stop looking," he commanded and draped the washcloth over his dick to cover it.

Obviously realizing the futility of that, he grasped it firmly in both hands to hide it. The tight grip combined with slick lather ratcheted up the sensation tenfold. Saige pumped her hips and gasped in pleasure as her knees went weak. Bracing both hands against the shower wall to remain upright, she caged Chase in as he released her dick and stood.

"Woman, you are a menace," he complained with a pissed off expression.

"Is it my fault that your dick likes my hands on it?" She shot back and was thrilled with the knowledge.

"It's a dick," he pointed out in an aggravated tone. "It gets excited when *I* touch it."

"Yeah, but I can guarantee it would like *my* touch better," she purred and decided to show him just how talented her hands were.

***

"What are you doing?" Chase demanded when she reached for the shampoo.

"Washing you," Saige replied with an innocent expression that he didn't buy for an instant. "Turn around."

He reluctantly turned his back on her and immediately regretted it. Her hands began to work shampoo through that damn gorgeous mane of hair, her fingers massaging his scalp. Hell yeah, it felt wonderful and her body responded to every touch. He breathed a sigh of relief that was short lived because the torment wasn't over yet.

Her soapy hands glided slowly over his shoulders and down his arms leaving gooseflesh in their wake. She washed his back with slow, circular motions before paying particular attention to the globes of his ass. Heat coiled low in his abdomen and he barely contained a groan. He should have known that Saige would turn this into something erotic.

Finally finished with his back, he turned as instructed and tilted his head back under the spray to rinse the shampoo away. Chase bit back a curse when she began the process again with conditioner. He hadn't had a clue what torment really was until she began to wash his front side, but now he knew.

Her touch was soft and gentle as she lathered his shoulders, as light as a feather while she kneaded both breasts, lightly tweaking the hardened nipples. By this point, his skin was so sensitive that even the soap suds trailing down his abdomen were shiver-inducing. The woman was going to kill him.

Every muscle tensed as she cupped his vagina. Her hand moved back and forth slowly, applying just the right amount of pressure to the sensitive bundle of nerves. One finger slid smoothly past lips swollen with need and he shuddered convulsively at the sensation. *Sweet Jesus.* He'd had no idea that a vagina was so sensitive.

Fighting to hold onto what little control he had left, Chase grasped her wrist and stilled the erotic motion. "That's enough," he insisted in a raspy voice.

"Just trying to be thorough," she said with a wicked grin and released him. "You know, Chase, this could be a once in a lifetime opportunity for you to really understand the female body. It's too bad you're too sexually repressed to take it."

He knew what she was trying to do and there was no way in hell it was happening. "Stop trying to goad me, Saige," he said in exasperation and rinsed the conditioner from his hair.

"I was actually being serious," she replied in a mocking tone. "The scientific community would be appalled at your lack of interest in experimentation, Professor."

"And documenting my experiences *as a woman* would make me a laughingstock," he derided as he grabbed a towel and dried her off briskly.

"Still, it is a fascinating concept," she mused as she took a towel and worked it gently through his hair. "It might even make you a better lover."

He gave her a quelling look and admitted, "I haven't had any complaints."

Saige merely gave him a look of disbelief and taunted, "Can you be passionate about anything other than science?"

With her, *hell yeah*, and he'd love to prove it. However, it wasn't in his best interest to admit it, so he wrapped her in the robe again and replied, "We're going to be late." Thankfully, she dropped the subject.

***

"Ow," Chase complained *again*.

"It wouldn't hurt if you'd hold still," she reminded him as she ran the brush through his hair.

"The hell it doesn't," he groused.

"You're such a wuss," she smirked and lifted another hank of hair under the stream of air from the blow dryer. "I do this every day."

"Masochist," he muttered. "This is even worse than the mascara."

"I told you not to blink," Saige reminded in amusement.

"You were coming at my eye with that thing. Blinking was a natural reaction," he defended.

"You make a terrible woman."

"Thank God for that," he replied with feeling.

"All right," she said in satisfaction as she laid the blow dryer aside and looked him over with a critical eye. "You're done." Chase rose and didn't even bother to look in the mirror so she asked, "Don't you want to see how you look?"

"I know how I look," he replied as he moved past her and into the bedroom. "I see you daily, remember?"

Yeah, and he was just as unimpressed now as he ever was, she thought glumly. Saige followed him into the bedroom and opened the closet door. She pulled out the business suit she had planned to wear and threw it on the bed. Removing a matching bra and panty set from the suitcase, she tossed them atop the pile.

"Get dressed."

He looked horrified at the idea. "You're not going to dress me?"

"I think a genius can figure out the intricacies of a bra clasp," she derided and sat down on the bed. She'd already suffered through the indignity of being dressed and groomed by him. No way in hell was she compounding it. He could deal with his revulsion for her nudity and dress his own damn self.

"Dammit, Saige, that's not the point," he complained.

"Yes, I know. You don't want to see me naked. I get it," she snapped. "Just close your damn eyes and put the clothes on Chase." Muttering imprecations under his breath, he did. Once he was dressed, she fished her shoes out of the suitcase. "Put these on."

***

Chase looked at the shoes dubiously. The heels had to be at least four inches tall. No way in hell was he wearing them. The last thing he needed was a twisted ankle. *Or a broken neck.* "Find something without a heel."

She laughed at that. "I don't own anything without a heel."

"If I break your neck, it's your fault," he grumbled as he took the shoes and tried to figure out how to put them on. There were straps going in every direction. Saige shook her head in exasperation and knelt down in front of him. She took the shoes and slid them onto his tiny little feet with practiced ease.

Chase stood slowly, wobbled a bit as he tried to get his balance and took a careful step. He would have face planted if she hadn't been there to steady him. "How the hell do you walk in these things?"

"If you think walking is hard, try dancing backward in them," she said dryly.

"So why do you wear them?" He asked curiously as she held his hand and led him around in a circle.

"Because guys think they're hot," she admitted.

He'd always thought so, but after experiencing the torture of trying to walk in the damn things, Chase was quickly revising his opinion. "A broken ankle is not hot," he pointed out.

"Then don't break one," she insisted as she led him into the lounge area. "Now get your ass in gear or we're gonna be late."

When she picked up her purse and draped it over her shoulder, he slid it back off. "Men don't carry purses."

"Well I need it, so *you'll* have to carry it," Saige insisted.

"What could you possibly need it for?" He demanded. "You're a man, remember?"

"You're not and that purse contains all the basic necessities," she pointed out. "Carry the damn thing."

"Fine," he growled and let her lead him out of the suite. "Why are you walking like you just got off of a horse."

"Feels like part of him is still down there," she muttered as she stepped into the elevator and jabbed a button. "How do you walk with all of this in the way?"

That brought a smirk to his face. "It requires proper placement." When she would have shoved her hand down the front of her pants, he grabbed it and demanded, "What are you doing?"

"Trying to find the proper placement."

"What did I tell you about touching?" He complained and was in the process of shoving his hand into the waistband when she caught it.

"Stop that. You can't just stick your hand in my pants and handle the goods whenever you feel like it," she growled.

"It's mine and I'll damn well handle it whenever I please," he growled right back.

"Ah, we'll take the next car," an amused voice said and Chase turned to see that the elevator door had opened and they had an audience. A very amused looking middle aged man, an older woman who looked scandalized and a teenage girl who gave him a wink and a thumbs up.

"Jesus Christ," Saige muttered as the doors slid shut. "Arrange your junk before the doors open again."

"Can't," he denied in resignation. "There's a security camera in the corner."

"I can't walk around like this," she groused and did a couple of squats, some kind of odd twerking motion and another squat.

"What the hell are you doing?" He demanded as he watched her bizarre gyrations.

"Finding the proper placement," she sighed in relief and flashed him a triumphant smirk.

The elevator doors opened and a man dressed in a military uniform was waiting for them. He stepped forward and shook Saige's hand. "Professor Marlowe, I'm Lieutenant Avery. I'm here to escort you to the Pentagon."

Chase stepped forward and extended his hand before she could flirt with the man. "Saige DeLancy, Lieutenant. I'm Professor Marlowe's assistant." The officer's handshake was professional, but the way his eyes roved over him was anything but. The bastard was attracted to Saige and that just pissed him off. "Shall we go?"

"If you'll follow me."

"You were rude," Saige hissed at him in an undertone.

"Keep your mouth shut," he hissed back and clutched her arm to keep his balance. The damn shoes would be the death of him if he wasn't careful. Chase stood corrected. Getting in the car in that short, tight assed skirt would do him in. Giving the lieutenant a glimpse of the hotter than hell red lace panties he wore wasn't happening.

After a quick mental calculation of the various angles, only one option seemed viable. He sat down with his back to the interior and swung both legs inside while pivoting his entire body into a forward position. He was pretty pleased with himself until Saige slid in beside him and muttered, "Graceful much?"

"I got in without showing your ass, didn't I?" He muttered back.

"Keep your knees together and try to act feminine," she hissed with a stern look.

Act feminine. How the hell was he supposed to do that? Chase was a dyed in the wool, one hundred percent heterosexual male. He had no clue how to act like a female. But he did know the woman beside him. He'd covertly watched her every move for years. He could do this. He just needed to behave like Saige.

God help him.

CHAPTER THREE

Three hours later, they arrived back at the hotel. When their escort got out to come around and open the door, Saige asked in an undertone, "It went great, so why are you scowling?"

Because he'd played the role of his PA too well. "Admiral Culverson pinched your ass," Chase informed her in disgust. After the initial shock of having his ass violated, he had realized that the admiral thought he'd pinched Saige. That had seriously pissed him off and he would have loved to punch the dirty old bastard's lights out.

"Did he now?" She asked in amusement. "Sorry I missed that. Those Navy men are hot."

That just pissed him off even more. The door opened and he grudgingly accepted the hand that Lieutenant Avery extended to assist him out of the car. Chase would have dismissed the man if he hadn't held on to his hand to say, "If you're ever in the area again, it would be my pleasure to give you a tour of DC, Ms. DeLancy."

Like hell, he would. Now that he knew she had a thing for Navy men, Chase decided to nip this situation in the bud. When she slid out of the car, he wrapped his arm around hers in a possessive manner and replied in a saccharine tone, "Thank you, Lieutenant. We'd love that, wouldn't we *sugar lips*?"

Saige merely glared at him in response. The officer assumed the look was meant for him and beat a hasty retreat. Task accomplished, Chase led her toward the lobby door.

"You are an ass," she hissed venomously. "Did it occur to you that I might have *wanted* a date with him?"

Damn right it had, which is exactly why he'd pulled that childish stunt. Jealousy really sucked. The confirmation that he'd been right fueled his temper even more and he snapped back, "You already have a revolving bedroom door. One less man won't make any difference."

"I can think of one that I could do without," she said stiffly.

***

Saige was incensed. *Damn the man.* How dare he say such a thing? Chase might as well have called her a whore. Yes, she dated a lot of men, but that sure as hell didn't mean that she'd had sex with them. Not to mention the main reason she dated so much was that she was trying *in vain* to find someone who could make her forget *him.*

She had thought that they were friends and it hurt more than she would ever admit to discover that he had such a low opinion of her. It also explained why the high and mighty Professor Marlowe didn't have any interest in her. Well the hell with him. She was sick and tired of loving a man who didn't give a damn about her.

Just as soon as she got her body back, she was going to quit.

They were halfway through the crowded lobby when Chase moaned and bent over double in pain. "I think there's something wrong with you."

"Why? Are you all right?" She asked anxiously. After pulling a stunt like that *he* deserved to suffer, but her body didn't.

"No. I've been having the most god awful abdominal cramps," he panted and braced his hands on his knees. "They just keep getting worse."

She slapped a hand against her forehead and exclaimed in a horrified tone, "Oh, my God! *I'm starting my period!*"

Fortunately, Chase didn't notice the startled looks that announcement received from the rather large group congregated in the lobby. He had paled a pasty white and groaned, "I'm gonna be sick."

"Nausea isn't a symptom," she said dryly.

"It is for a man," he assured her as he stood upright and placed a hand against his abdomen. "Listen, I can't deal with the whole tampon thing so you'd better figure out how to stop this."

Saige stared at him as if he'd lost his mind. "Yeah. Women have been working on that one since the dawn of time," she snarked and led him toward the elevators. "Let me know if you figure it out, genius."

"Why am I craving chocolate?" He complained.

"That *is* a symptom," she said in amusement as they stepped inside the car.

"It's not funny, dammit," he replied in a petulant tone.

"Oh, it is," she differed. It really, really was. PMS was a bitch after all and if any man deserved it, Chase Marlowe did. "Finally a man gets to suffer through menstrual cramps. The only thing better would be labor pains. Too bad I'm not pregnant."

An appalled expression covered his face. "You are an evil woman."

"Yeah, but I know how to make you feel better."

He groaned in pain again and said, "If you can do that you're getting a raise. A *big* raise."

It was too little, too late. Saige didn't want a raise. She wanted a new job, far away from the insufferable ass who'd broken her heart. Her smile was saccharine sweet when she reached inside the purse he carried and extracted a zippered leather pouch. "This is a PMS pouch. It contains everything you need. Feel free to indulge, *sugar lips*."

That said, she walked out of the elevator and left him to fend for himself.

***

Holding onto the wall like a drunken sailor on leave allowed Chase to make his way back to their suite without breaking an ankle. When he got his body back the first thing he was going to do was wring her neck. The second thing was to invent something to alleviate menstrual cramps. The pain he felt was excruciating.

After digging through the contents of the oversized bag for an eternity, he finally found the key card and let himself in. Muttering foul imprecations under his breath, he wobbled unsteadily to the couch and dropped onto it. A moan of pure anguish escaped his lips as he flopped over onto his side and drew his knees up against his chest.

Curling into the fetal position provided a modicum of relief even if it was completely undignified. However, Chase wasn't a man with a masculine image to protect right then. He was a woman whose fragile little body was in agony. Hoping the contents of Saige's *PMS pouch* would help, he sat upright with a whimper.

Removing those damn shoes was priority one. After several fumbling attempts with the tiny buckle, his feet were finally free of the torture devices. Task complete, he opened the pouch and peered warily inside at the contents. The purple and gold foil wrapped spheres looked like candy. A sniff test confirmed it was chocolate.

Chase unwrapped one, popped it into his mouth and bit down. The decadent creamy filling exploded onto his taste buds and he moaned in ecstasy. Oh, man. *It was so good.* Which was surprising since he didn't normally care for chocolate. He smoothed out the wrapper and discovered this little bite of heaven was called a dark chocolate truffle.

Yeah. He'd definitely be stocking up on these.

Licking his lips, he reached into the pouch and removed a plastic sandwich bag. It contained several packages of lavender chamomile tea. Yuck. He wasn't that desperate. *Yet.* There was also a bottle of ibuprofen so he popped two into his mouth and swallowed them dry. Another truffle helped wash them down.

Further investigation revealed a package containing a thermal heat patch. He tore into that bad boy and rose gingerly to his feet. Chase yanked the tight tailed skirt up to his waist and pressed the adhesive patch against his abdomen. He couldn't help noticing how silky smooth her skin felt beneath his fingertips. Or how sexy the red panties were.

God, he was a sick bastard to be drooling over Saige's panties at a time like this.

Snatching the skirt back into place, he sat back down and continued his quest through the bag. Down at the bottom were white bullet-shaped objects and innocuous square packages wrapped in pink and purple plastic. Realizing that these were the dreaded feminine hygiene products, a shudder of revulsion shook him.

Chase placed everything back into the pouch, stuffed it in the purse and went in search of his nemesis. He found her in the bathroom putting her toiletries into a case. "What are you doing?" He asked curiously.

"Packing," came the clipped response.

"For what?" He queried in confusion since they weren't scheduled to return home until tomorrow.

"There's a flight leaving in two hours, so I changed our reservations," she explained as she zipped the case.

"That may not be a good idea," he pointed out and followed her back into the bedroom. "We don't know if proximity will affect the reversal process."

"I don't care," she snapped and zipped her suitcase with more force than necessary. "I'm going home with or without you, Chase."

He might be the one with cramps, but Saige was definitely having the mood swings. Something had put a bee up her ass and he wasn't going to argue about it. Chase would rather be able to access his lab in case this situation didn't resolve itself by morning. Not that he knew what the hell to do if it didn't, but at least he'd be able to experiment.

Besides, he wasn't about to let her out of his sight until they switched back. If anything happened to Saige he wouldn't have a body to revert back to. Just the thought of being stuck in a woman's body permanently terrified him, but it was the thought of losing *her* that galvanized him into action. "I'll go pack," he said by way of agreement and left the room.

***

Saige had never liked flying and she seemed more antsy than usual this time. When they had hit a particularly rough patch of turbulence, he'd thought she was going to jump out of her seat. Chase had tried to take her hand in a comforting gesture, but she'd snatched it away from him like he'd scalded her. The look she had given him had been scathing, to say the least.

Women.

In spite of the fact that he'd been one for most of the day, he still had no concept of how their minds worked. The same *could not* be said of their bodies, unfortunately. He had come to the determination that the craving for chocolate was strictly for the endorphin, serotonin, and dopamine release since it had helped improve his mood.

The heat patch had eased the cramping a minuscule amount, but the ibuprofen was useless.

This was morphine level pain.

Out of sheer desperation, Chase had invoked the name of every god, deity and divine being he could think of in the hopes that the hygiene products didn't become necessary. Because if they did... his psyche would be scarred permanently. He also realized that he was turning into a fucking drama queen.

Once they landed, he had driven them directly to the lab. Saige had brooded silently while he'd drawn blood and run a battery of tests to determine if anything about their physical compositions had changed. The EEG showed normal brain wave patterns and the MRI didn't reveal any abnormalities. So far everything appeared to be perfectly normal.

If he disregarded the fact that their conscious minds had somehow swapped bodies. Yeah. Chase was still trying to wrap his head around that one. No pun intended. Ninety-five percent of brain activity was beyond conscious awareness, which meant that approximately five percent of their brain function had jumped ship.

Because a fortune cookie had proved prophetic.

Jesus Christ.

The alternate reality theory was sounding better by the minute.

"All of the results are conclusive," he informed Saige after he ran the comprehensive metabolic panel of their blood for the second time. "There is nothing physically wrong with us."

"Right," she replied scathingly as she stopped her mindless pacing to glare at him. "That totally explains why I have a dick."

He sighed wearily and ran a hand through his hair, cursing under his breath when his fingers got tangled in those damn curls *again*. When she slung that oversized purse over her shoulder and headed for the door, he demanded, "Where the hell do you think you're going?"

"I quit," she replied and kept right on walking.

"Saige," he said in exasperation as he followed her out into the hall in his bare feet. The aggravating woman was going to drive him insane. There was no way in hell that he could let her quit. He'd never get anything accomplished without her badgering and not seeing her every day would be unbearable. "You can't quit."

"The hell I can't." He caught up with her at the elevator and grasped her arm. She turned to face him and snapped, "Don't touch me."

***

When the elevator doors opened, Chance Marlowe saw his twin brother and Chase's assistant standing in front of them. Wondering why the hell his brother was carrying a *purse*, he stepped back so they could enter the car. It didn't take long to wish he'd gotten out instead. The two of them were immersed in a heated argument, as usual.

"What the hell is your problem?" Saige demanded in annoyance.

"Seriously?" His brother fired back angrily as he jabbed the button for the first floor. "For starters, I woke up in your bed this morning. Correction, I woke up in *you*." Well, damn. Chase had finally had sex with his hotter than hell assistant. It was about fucking time, but it didn't sound like he was pleased with the decision. *Dumbass.*

"After that, you insisted on holding my dick *while I peed* and *forced me* to take a shower with you," Chase accused and looked pissed as hell about it. Well, Chance couldn't really blame him there. Having a chick hold your dick while you peed might be taking things a little too far, but the shower sounded like fun.

"Jesus Christ", his assistant muttered and raked a hand through her hair, getting her fingers tangled in the thick curls.

"Then you got pissed because the admiral pinched my ass and intentionally scared off the lieutenant when he asked me out," his brother continued hotly while Chance's eyebrows shot to his hairline and his mouth fell open in shock. *Holy fucking shit!* His twin was bi-sexual? Well, that certainly explained the purse.

"But the final straw was when you called me a *whore*!" Chase all but shouted.

Having managed to finally get her fingers untangled, Saige vehemently denied, "I did *not* call you a whore!"

"No?" His brother demanded angrily. "Then I suppose that crack about my bedroom having a revolving door and one less man not making a difference was your idea of a joke?"

Chase with a revolving bedroom door? The idea would have been laughable a half hour ago. Now that he knew his brother's sexual proclivities had taken a walk on the wild side, he wasn't so sure. Because it damn sure sounded like Saige knew a hell of a lot more about his brother's sex life than Chance wanted to.

"It wasn't… I didn't mean…" she stammered and looked as lost as Chance felt.

"I don't give a damn," he said forcefully and Chance hastily stepped aside before his brother walked right through him when the doors opened. He stared incredulously when Chase stopped in the lobby to do a couple of squats and some bizarre twerking motion. "If this nightmare isn't over by morning I'm getting castrated."

"Don't you dare touch my dick!" Saige yelled after him.

To which his brother yelled back, "Fuck you!"

"Jesus Christ," the assistant muttered in exasperation and raked both hands through her hair. When all of her fingers got tangled in the curls she cursed a blue streak and began trying to twist them loose.

Realizing that she was making a bigger mess of it, Chance stepped forward and offered, "Need some help?"

"I need a lobotomy," Saige snapped viciously but stood still and let him untwist the curls.

He laughed lightly and said, "My brother can be a pain in the ass."

"Fuck you, too," she growled.

It was all Chance could do not to laugh. She looked like a pissed off kitten and it was adorable. If he hadn't been head over heels for his own assistant, he might have given his brother some competition. "I guess now isn't a good time to ask how the meeting with the Joint Chiefs went," he commented wryly.

"It went fine," Saige said gruffly. "I'll be giving them a live demonstration as soon as they can fit it into their schedule."

"*You* will?" He asked in surprise.

She gave him a hard look and said sarcastically, "Yeah. *Me*. Chase Marlowe, your twin brother. The one who's been stuck in a woman's body since I woke up this morning. The one who's man-hungry assistant just walked out of here with *my dick*."

Chance was staring at the woman as if she'd lost her mind. Actually, that was exactly what he was thinking. Oh, hell. *Was this schizophrenia?* Or one of those multiple personality disorder things? *Shit.* Chase would know, but the dumbass had left him here to deal with *Insane Jane* by himself. "Uh…" Yeah. He was at a loss how to deal with this situation.

The woman folded her arms over her ample chest and said, "You got drunk your freshman year in college and wound up with a pink butterfly tattooed on your ass. Once you sobered up you got a red dragon to cover it."

What. The. Fuck? Chance was stunned speechless. There was no way in hell that Saige could know that. *No one* except his brother knew and Chase would never tell. *Never.* "How the hell do you..."

"Because I'm your *brother*," Saige said impatiently. "Don't ask me how it happened because I don't know. What I do know is that this... *debacle* should reverse itself at midnight. I hope."

"You're really Chase," he said in bewilderment and was trying to work it out in his head. *His brother was a woman.* So that meant... "That was Saige? In *your* body?"

"Yes," was confirmed on a weary sigh.

"So... you're not bi-sexual," he deduced. If the outraged look on her face was any indication, that would be a no.

"Fuck no," Saige, er... *Chase* denied hotly. Then he grabbed his abdomen and complained in a petulant tone, "I'm a woman, and I'm starting my period."

Chance paled to ash and admitted, "Think I'd prefer it if you were bi."

CHAPTER FOUR

A persistent hammering, interspersed with the doorbell buzzing finally annoyed Saige enough that she opened the door. She leaned indolently against the doorframe, a glass of scotch in her hand. "What do you want, Chase?" She asked irritably.

"You took the purse," he complained. "I didn't have the keys to your apartment."

"So you came here," she deduced and took a sip of whiskey.

"It is my home," he pointed out reasonably.

"Right now it's mine," she reminded him with a smirk. "Just like your dick."

"Saige," he growled in warning.

She turned and walked back out onto the rooftop patio to settle comfortably into a chaise lounge. Saige had been sitting out there enjoying the view of the city lights and catching a nice buzz before he arrived. She was not in the mood to argue. Not anymore. She just wanted this fiasco to be over so she could move on to the next phase of her life.

A life that did not include Professor Chase Marlowe.

Funny how that didn't hurt as much as it had an hour ago. The scotch was numbing the pain nicely. When he sat down in the chair next to her, she commented, "I love this view. If I lived here I'd sleep in this spot."

"I have the same view from my bed," he pointed out. "And it's more comfortable."

She laughed and wagged her finger at him. "If you were anyone else, I'd think that was an invitation," she didn't mind admitting. "But coming from you I'm sure it's just a statement of fact."

"Why would you think that?" He queried.

"Because the great Professor Marlowe would never sully his linens with a woman of my ilk," she said bitterly and took another sip.

***

Chase felt a pang of anguish straight through his heart because he'd hurt her. He'd lashed out in jealousy and hurt the one woman in the world that he never wanted to cause pain. He needed to fix this and the only way he knew how was to tell her the truth. He took the glass from her and drained the contents in one swallow.

"I'm sorry. That crack about the revolving door was uncalled for and I only said it because I was jealous," he confessed and sat the tumbler aside. Saige snorted in disbelief and shot him a venomous look. "The only reason I've never invited you to share my bed is because I wouldn't be able to let you leave it."

She laughed mirthlessly and replied, "I'm good, Chase, but not *that* good."

He bit back a curse and bared his soul. "Dammit, Saige, I'm trying to tell you that I love you," he said in exasperation. "If I ever made you mine I'd fight like hell to keep you and I know that's not what you want."

She stared at him for a minute before she said, "Damn. That's some good scotch. Because it sounded like you said…"

"I love you," he repeated solemnly. "It's not the scotch. And we're not in an alternate reality. This is as real as it gets. I'm in love with you, Saige. I have been for a very long time."

***

Saige stared at him in astonishment as it sank in. *Chase loved her.* He loved her! Holy Hannah. She swung her legs off the side of the chaise and sat facing him. "I've been in love with you for years," she admitted. "And all those men…"

"Are not important," he interrupted with a scowl.

"Just because I dated them doesn't mean I had sex with them," she finished doggedly. "I was trying to find someone who could make me forget about you."

"Did you?"

"No, Chase," she denied softly. "No one compares to you."

His smile was heartbreakingly beautiful when he asked, "Would you like to see the view from my bed?"

"Is that an invitation?" She asked hopefully.

"Of a sort," he confirmed. "I've waited a long time to make love to you, sweetheart. When I get my hands on this gorgeous body you're going to be in it. Tonight, I just want to know what it's like to fall asleep with you in my arms."

Her heart melted at the romantic gesture. "It sounds perfect," she agreed.

Chase rose and helped her to her feet. Her hand still held in his, he led her into his bedroom where they undressed each other and snuggled together in the center of the bed. In spite of the boner she sported, Saige was perfectly content to just lay there holding him. It was so sweet and intimate. She felt… *loved* and it was a wonderful feeling.

Although she was certain that the sex was going to be *phenomenal*.

Which brought to mind another dilemma. "Chase?"

"Hmm?" He murmured in a tone of sheer contentment.

"What happens if we don't switch back?"

"I start working on a cure for menstrual cramps tomorrow morning."

She laughed and slapped his arm lightly. "I'm serious."

"So was I," he admitted and tightened his hold on her protectively. "Knowing that you hurt like this is all the incentive I need to make it a top priority."

"Aww. That's so sweet," she said with a huge smile. "Now stop trying to distract me and answer the question."

The bark of laughter gave him away. "You know me too well."

"Mmm. I hope to know you much better as soon as we switch bodies again," she assured him.

"Which is exactly why we *have* to switch," he agreed.

"But if we don't?"

"Then I guess you'll have to teach me the proper way to deep throat," he said with a devilish grin. Saige lifted her head and stared at him in astonishment. Chase rarely joked, but when he did that delightfully wicked sense of humor never failed to surprise her. "Well, I can't let my dick be deprived and I've been told it's not as easy as it looks."

To which they both burst into unrestrained laughter.

***

Chase came awake slowly, the events of the previous day filtering through his brain like a bad movie on fast forward. He'd been trapped in a woman's body. *And his dick had been missing.* His hand immediately reached for his favorite appendage and encountered neatly trimmed pubic hair, *but no dick*. His heart damn near stopped.

Not again!

Eyes popping open, he stared wild-eyed at the woman in his arms. *Saige!* He was holding Saige. His hand covering *her* vagina. Then that meant... they had switched back into their own bodies! *Halle-fucking-lujah!* He breathed a sigh of relief and felt all the tension leave his body in a rush.

At least it had before he realized that he'd woken up with the woman he loved in his arms. *And that his dick was still in perfect working order*. Being pressed tightly against her hot little ass had it as hard as granite. *Hell, yeah*. Chase couldn't think of a better way to celebrate than making love to Saige.

Then he remembered those damn menstrual cramps and his dick shrank to half mast. He sighed heavily in resignation. At least he could cuddle her. Women seemed to like it and he for damn sure loved the feel of her body pressed so intimately against his. Now that he had her in his bed, Chase had no intentions of letting her out of it again.

Saige was finally his.

A smile of satisfaction on his lips, he placed a tender kiss against her shoulder. She grunted sleepily in response. "Good morning, sweetheart," he breathed softly against her ear and she muttered something incomprehensible. Smiling in amusement, Chase nudged her tight little ass with his pelvis and received an elbow to the ribs.

"Ow," he complained and shifted back away from the sharp appendage. "You're a vicious little thing in the morning, aren't you?" She growled something completely unintelligible and scooted back toward him until her back was once again pressed against his front. He smiled because even grumpy, Saige was still adorable.

"Sweetheart, I have a dick," he said next to her ear. "And you don't."

***

Wide awake now, Saige bolted upright in bed, smacking her head into a brick on the way. "Ouch," she yelped and lifted a hand to rub her aching head. A glance beside her revealed Chase lying next to her holding his chin and eyeing her balefully. Her eyes trailed downward and Holy Hannah! His chest and abs were just as drool worthy as she remembered.

Wait. If he was *beside her* then that meant… one look down revealed her own body. *"Yes,"* she cried in exultation and flashed him a brilliant smile. "I'm a woman!"

"A dangerous one," he complained and worked his jaw from side to side.

"Only before coffee," she said in amusement since the brick had to have been his carved from stone chin. Twisting around as agile as a cat, she placed a kiss on it. Before she could blink, Chase had flipped them and she was lying beneath him. His forearms bracketed her head as he held the bulk of his weight off of her.

"Good morning, sweetheart," he said with a smile so wicked that it sent tingles down her spine.

She draped her arms over his broad shoulders, slid her legs over his and arched into him. "Mmm. It is now," she replied in a throaty purr and lifted her head to place kisses along his jaw.

Chase groaned as if he were in pain. "Saige, we can't," he said in a tone filled with regret.

The steel rod currently pressed against her clit in the most delightful manner assured her that they most assuredly could. "The hell we can't. *You* have a dick. *I* have a vagina. Insert part A into part B, Professor."

He arched one eyebrow and said dryly, "You also have your period."

Saige snorted a laugh. "The cramps start three days before my period, so I'm safe until tomorrow," she confessed. A split second later his mouth had adhered to hers in a toe curling kiss that she'd been waiting three years for. And it had definitely been worth the wait! Because Chase didn't just kiss her.

He *devoured* her.

The kiss was a claiming. A blatant display of masculine need and she reveled in his mastery. It would seem that he *could* be passionate about something other than science. Man, could he! The way he was making love to her mouth, she could easily orgasm from his kiss alone. *Oh, hell yeah.* The sex was definitely going to be phenomenal.

When he released her lips, she pulled in a much-needed gulp of oxygen and opened eyes laden with desire. Every bit of the air rushed right back out of her lungs when she saw his face. Chase looked hungry. Starved, in fact. And he was staring down at her with an expression filled with raw lust.

Shivers danced down her spine because his eyes, those intelligent brown eyes, were filled with all the love she'd ever wanted. He cupped her cheek in one hand and lowered his head to place the tenderest of kisses on her lips. Chase's tone was reverent when he confessed, "I love you, Saige DeLancey."

Tears of joy filled her eyes and she whispered, "I love you, Chase Marlowe."

***

His heart swelled to overflowing as he gazed down at the love shining in her sage green eyes. The golden curls splayed across his pillow, her cheeks flushed with desire. Saige was simply radiant. "This is how I wanted my first time seeing you naked to be," he said solemnly as his fingertips traced the line of her neck to her shoulder.

A wry smile curved her lips. "I'm sorry my wish ruined that for you."

His smile became wicked as he admitted, "It wasn't all your fault. I made the same wish three times, too."

"Shut up," she said in surprise and smacked his shoulder. "What did you wish?"

"That I could have your gorgeous body," Chase confessed.

After a moment of stunned silence, Saige laughed merrily and asked, "Well, it's all yours now so what are you gonna do with it?"

"Kiss, taste and touch every inch of you," he said as his lips skimmed down her neck before licking a trail back up to her ear. "I've got three years of fantasies to enact."

"Then I suggest you get started ASAP and stay on task," she informed him in her bossy PA tone.

Chase hovered above her, his eyes locked with hers, his expression deadly serious. "Sweetheart, I need you to keep me focused and on task *in the lab*," he assured her seriously. "But this is the one place I will not be rushed. I'm going to take my time and lavish you with all the pleasure that you can handle. Understand?"

Those sage green eyes had gotten bigger with every word he'd uttered and were staring back at him a bit bemused. A muffled squeak escaped her lips as she nodded her head vigorously. "Good," he said confidently. "Let's see how much of my undivided attention you can take before you start begging instead of demanding."

It didn't take long, he realized in satisfaction. Saige was so responsive to his slightest touch. Her body came alive under his skillful ministrations and she broke within minutes. Although she did alternate between pleading for release and demanding it. It was cute as hell, but she'd learn quickly that he had meant what he'd said.

There was no rushing this.

Her first orgasm came while he was focused solely on her breasts. Well, he was a genius after all. Chase knew every way there was to bring a woman to climax with and without penetration. From a multitude of positions. Yeah. He was showing off, but she wasn't complaining about it.

Just the opposite.

Saige was practically purring in contentment. Oh, man. He liked her like this. All soft and pliant, a sated smile curving those luscious lips. And he really liked being the lucky bastard who'd caused it. After a kiss that left them both breathless, Chase flipped her onto her stomach and paid homage to the absolute perfection of her ass.

His fingertips trailed over the creamy globes, his touch as soft and fleeting as the brush of butterfly wings. Gooseflesh pebbled over skin as smooth as satin. Sleekly toned muscles quivered under his delicate touch. "Mmm," Saige murmured contentedly, a hint of amusement evident in her tone. "You're such a tease."

His hand delved between her parted thighs, his fingers sliding unerringly into her heated depths. Her gasp of pleasure was music to his ears. "No teasing," he promised. "Just pleasure." True to his word, he brought her to a second shattering climax using only the skill and dexterity of his fingers.

"Chase," she panted breathlessly as he rolled her onto her back again.

"Damn right it's Chase," he said smugly as he knelt on the floor at the foot of the bed. He grasped her legs and pulled her ass to the edge. Spreading her thighs wide, his hungry gaze raked hotly over her quivering flesh. His thumb lightly traced the slit between her swollen lips. "You're so wet for me," he said hoarsely.

Consumed by a compulsion to taste, he lowered his head and licked slowly. Her ass lifted off the bed in response. She tasted like sin and sugar and he had to have more. Placing his hands around her hips, Chase rose while pivoting, fell backward onto the bed, and landed so that Saige was sitting astride his head. Yeah. He was still showing off.

The move startled a laugh out of her and she demanded in amusement, "What are you... *oh!*" It didn't take a genius to figure that out. If the position hadn't been obvious enough, his mouth removed any misconceptions. Chase locked his hands around her hips and held her in place as he devoured her.

Saige mewled in pleasure, bucked her hips and sank her nails into his scalp. She begged, pleaded, whimpered and cursed him, but he was unrelenting in his determination. Then she shattered with climax number three, a hoarse cry wrenched from her throat. She collapsed bonelessly atop him, her entire body quivering with aftershocks.

Chase rolled them and shifted up so they were lying facing each other, their heads on the pillows once again. He brushed the tangled mane of curls from her face and stared at the most beautiful sight he'd ever seen. Saige, *his Saige*, looked wanton and sated and so goddamn beautiful that his heart twisted.

"Wow," she breathed. "That was... wow."

"Sweetheart, we've only just begun," he said with a devilish smile and saw her eyes widen in shocked disbelief. *Challenge accepted.* It was time to show his woman exactly how much he wanted her. And prove just how much pleasure he could give.

***

Saige was completely limp with exhaustion and satiated beyond anything she had ever known. She had wondered what it would be like to be on the receiving end of his laser-like focus, and now she knew. *Holy Hannah, it was beyond phenomenal.* He had brought her to one glorious orgasm after another until she'd lost count.

Chase was relentless in his desire to please her and he showed no evidence of ending his single-minded pursuit. He was so completely absorbed in making her climax that he'd ignored his own release completely. His body was slick with sweat, his muscles trembling, and still, he kept his focus entirely on her. His stamina was incredible.

"Chase, please," she pleaded for the millionth time. "I want you in me. *I need you in me.* Please, Chase. Make love to me now."

Her words fell on deaf ears, just like they did when he was absorbed in one of his projects at the lab. So she was going to have to do something drastic to get his attention just like she did at work. His dick was so engorged that it was almost purple and looked painful as hell. Saige lightly grasped it and heard him hiss, either in pain or pleasure she couldn't tell.

"Sweetheart, don't," he choked out rawly and gently removed her hand.

"You've spent over two hours on foreplay, Chase," Saige informed him. "I want you in me right fucking now."

He arched an eyebrow and asked, "Didn't I tell you that I wouldn't be rushed?"

"Yes, but if you don't deal with that erection soon, your dick is going to explode," she pointed out in exasperation.

"You've got a point," he agreed with a rueful smile.

A wicked smile curved her lips as she offered, "I can show you the proper way to deep throat."

His gaze lowered to her lips and regret shown in his eyes. "Not this time," he refused. "I wouldn't last long enough to enjoy it."

"You might not last long," she confirmed with a naughty smile. "But I guarantee you *would* enjoy it."

"Next time," he promised and wiped every thought from her head with another one of those mind drugging kisses he was so expert at. "I want this to be special, Saige."

"It is," she assured him with what little brain power she could muster. "Because it's our first time together."

That must have appeased him because he settled into position between her thighs. "I love you," Chase said solemnly as his eyes locked with hers.

"I love you more," she countered with a smile.

He entered her in slow, measured increments that took her breath away. "Holy shit," Chase breathed when he was fully seated and lowered his forehead to hers. "You're so wet and tight."

"And you're so big and hard," she sighed happily.

When he began to move, his thrusts were deliberately slow and easy. From the tension that she felt in him, Saige could tell that he was fighting to keep a tight rein on himself. The hell with that. Chase was always so controlled. She wanted him unleashed, wild and as desperate for her as she'd been for him.

She snaked a hand between their bodies and cupped his balls. He froze mid-thrust and choked out, "What are you doing?"

"Let go of your control, Chase," she urged and gently massaged the twin orbs. "Show me your passion."

"No," he grated between clenched teeth. "Gotta feel you come around me."

She laughed lightly at that. "Oh, honey, you've worn me out," Saige assured him. "I don't have another orgasm left in me." Something flared in his eyes and his face took on the determined expression that she knew so well. Uh, oh. She'd done it now. Chase had taken that as a challenge, the one thing he could not seem to resist.

"I think you do," he said seriously as he lifted one of her legs up until her knee touched her chest. "Maybe even two."

A shiver of anticipation danced down her spine as she released his balls. "Give it your best shot," she challenged with a naughty smile.

Damned if he didn't.

Chase began a series of fast and deep thrusts that almost blew the top off of her head. Then he switched to slow and shallow thrusts before shifting gears again. The heat began to build in her abdomen, tension rising and falling, rising and falling. He held her poised on the edge of release until she was a shaking mass of need.

"Now… now… now… *please… God… now…*" she chanted in time with his thrusts. And just when she thought she couldn't stand another second of the delicious torture, Chase bit down gently on her nipple. The orgasm exploded through her body like a Tsunami hell bent on complete annihilation.

Saige screamed his name as she locked her arms and legs around him and held on for dear life. But his relentless thrusts never slowed. If anything he doubled his efforts and began to pound his body into hers as if his life depended on it. *Yes!* His control had finally snapped and *oh my God* phenomenal didn't even begin to describe it!

Much to her astonishment, when his climax came, it triggered yet another one in her as well. They collapsed together, panting and trembling with aftershocks, both too weak and winded to speak. Spent, exhausted and completely content, they just lay there holding each other, basking in the euphoria of ecstasy.

"I won't be able to walk for a week," she said when she finally had the air to breathe again.

"Doesn't matter. I'm not letting you out of bed for at least that long," he countered as he shifted them onto their sides.

"Yeah, you will," she said in amusement.

"Not happening," he assured her.

"You forgot my period," Saige reminded.

"Fuck," Chase groused in defeat.

She laughed merrily and hugged him tightly. "I love you."

"Love you more," he swore and kissed her forehead tenderly.

"Do not."

"Do so."

"Prove it."

He studied her for a minute and said, "I'd willingly suffer labor pains for you."

"Seriously?" Saige asked in amusement. "Because you didn't handle menstrual cramps that well."

"Which should prove how serious I am," Chase agreed.

What it proved was that he was the most loveable man she'd ever known and her heart melted all over again. "Okay," she agreed smugly. "I'd let you suffer labor pains for me, but that doesn't prove you love me more."

"Does too."

"Does not."

"Does."

"It does not because it can't happen," she pointed out.

"It could," he reminded her dryly.

"*If* I were pregnant," she conceded.

"You will be," he said as if it were a foregone conclusion. "After we've been married a couple of years."

Saige's heart stuttered to a halt before kick starting into overdrive. "Married?" She whispered in shock.

"I told you that once I had you in my bed I'd never let you go," Chase said seriously. "That means marriage, kids, the whole nine yards."

"Yes," she said as tears of joy filled her eyes. "I want it all."

"Good," he agreed with the devilish smile that first stole her heart. "Maybe this will convince my brother I'm not bi-sexual."

"You're not what?"

EPILOGUE
Three Years Later…

"Chase, wake up," he heard through a haze of sleep.

"Hmm," he responded groggily.

"The sheets are wet. I think my water broke," she said with a bit more urgency. His brain cleared instantly and Chase was wide awake now. *Saige was having their baby!* His eyes popped open and in the pre-dawn light he stared up at… *his face?*

What. The. Fuck?

"Honey, you finally get to prove that you love me more," she said and bit her lip anxiously. "Because I'm pretty sure you're in labor."

The most god awful pain gripped his abdomen and rolled through his body in a tidal wave of pure agony. Chase looked down in horror and saw his distended belly contort in sync with the contraction. He was in labor. Holy fucking hell! *He was in labor!* Sheer terror gripped his soul. *"No. No, no, noooooo!"*

The End

TONYA BROOKS

SHE'S MY
Obsession

I BOINKED THE BOSS SERIES

SHE'S MY OBSESSION
I Boinked The Boss Series

TONYA BROOKS

CHAPTER ONE

Chance Marlowe glanced through the open door at his sexy as hell assistant *again*. It seemed that he spent half of his time at the office staring at her. Hell, he'd even moved his desk so he'd have an optimal view. God, what that woman did to him. Reva Blaine had the kind of curvaceous body that a man couldn't help staring at.

And fantasizing about.

His dad would have said she was built like a brick house. The old man would have also told him that he was a damn fool for not making her his. Chance would love nothing better *if* she wasn't his employee. The most loyal, dedicated and hard working employee he had. But he'd replace her in a minute if he thought she was interested in him.

Brother would he.

Because the woman had become an obsession. The most erotic fantasies he'd ever had were centered around her. Ms. Blaine looked so prim and proper in her knee length pencil skirts and silky blouses. And those reading glasses set his balls on fire. When her big blue eyes peered at him over the top of them, he forgot his own name.

And sprang a boner that would crush granite.

His fingers itched to let her raven black hair down and run his fingers through it. To strip away her pristine façade and discover the passionate woman that he knew she kept hidden inside. Because Reva amped the good girl with a naughty streak image to the max with the fuck me shoes she always wore. God, he loved those freaking shoes.

Almost as much as he loved her.

Hell, it was impossible not to love her. She was beautiful, intelligent, too sexy for her own good, and so damn sweet that Chance wanted to gobble her up. Starting with slow, delicious licks to her delicate neck before he nibbled every luscious curve. Unfortunately, the possibility of that happening was slim to none.

But he'd promised himself if Reva ever gave him the slightest bit of encouragement, that nothing would stop him from making her his. *Permanently.* In the meantime, he tormented himself by watching her covertly. And listening to the snorts, sighs and grumbling noises she made while she worked.

God how he loved the sexy little sounds she made. At the moment, she was draped over her desk fast asleep and it actually sounded like she was purring. He stood and adjusted the steel rod in his pants. Chance needed to wake his little sex kitten and make sure she got safely tucked into bed for the night.

Preferably *his.*

And not just for the night.

CHAPTER TWO

Reva Blaine was exhausted, mentally and physically. If she didn't love her job so much, she'd quit. Correction. If she wasn't madly in love with her sinfully handsome boss, she'd quit. The sad thing was that the man had absolutely no idea. Truth be told, she wasn't even sure he knew her first name since he always called her *Ms. Blaine*.

Gah. Unrequited love really sucked.

She wasn't shy by any means and had no problem letting a man know when she was interested, but Chance Marlowe wasn't just a man. *He was a freaking god among men.* He was blessed with cover model good looks and a body made for sin. Not to mention the wickedest smile she'd ever had the pleasure of seeing.

A sigh of longing slid past her lips. Her boss was absolute perfection and as far out of her league as the Maserati he drove. Not that she was ground beef, but she wasn't exactly filet mignon either. Reva was petite and a little too curvy thanks to the second greatest love of her life; chocolate.

One of her favorite fantasies was coating Chance's muscular body in dark chocolate gooiness and licking him clean. *Have mercy.* Just the thought was enough to elevate her body temperature to dangerous degrees. Though the possibility of it ever happening was about as likely as the Pope opening a brothel in the Vatican.

So, yeah. Unrequited love sucked hairy balls.

Shoving the depressing thought into a mental box along with her dreams of wearing a bikini, she focused on the report she'd been proofreading. The blinking cursor separated into two, did the Macarena and merged back into one. The darn thing was mocking her and she was too tired to care. She really needed a good night's sleep.

Preferably curled up in Chance's arms.

In Chance's bed.

Reva snorted inelegantly. Forget sleep. If she ever had the opportunity to share that man's bed, the last thing that either of them would get was sleep. *Gah*. Her mind had wandered *again*. Though it wasn't hard when the report she was proofreading was so boring. The darn thing was filled with technical terms that made no sense to her.

Then again, the majority of what went on at the company didn't. Marlowe Labs was a research and development company that specialized in all kinds of scientific projects. Chance ran the business while his twin brother Chase was the freaking genius who ran the lab. They were fraternal twins, but looks were not their only differences.

Chase was totally focused on his projects, intense and quick tempered. Chance was equally driven, but with a laid back, fun loving personality. They were like daylight and dark. Yin and yang. Squash and strawberries. Complete opposites. Thank heavens. Reva didn't think her heart could take being around two of Chance on a daily basis.

Gah. Unrequited love sucked big, hairy donkey balls.

Forcing her attention back to the dancing cursor, she read the blurred words one more time. The technical mumbo jumbo still didn't make a bit of sense, but at least there were no typos or grammar errors. With a sigh of relief, she hit print. A glance at the clock revealed it was nine pm. Great. She'd put in *another* twelve hour day.

Chance was lucky that she loved her job. Correction. That she loved *him*. Reva removed her glasses and laid them aside to massage her tired eyes. The printer was chugging away and she knew it would take a while to print the massive document. Unable to resist, she folded her arms atop the desk and lowered her cheek onto them.

She'd rest while it printed. Her heavy eyelids lowered of their own volition. For just a few minutes. Her breathing slowed. A little break was all she needed. Her muscles went lax. Just a few minutes to get her second wind. Her brain went into hibernation mode. Within moments, Reva was sound asleep and dreaming of Chance.

"Mmm," she purred in contentment.

She felt his fingertips lightly caress her cheek, the touch so warm and gentle. A sigh of pleasure escaped her parted lips. Reva opened her eyes, lifted her head and saw him kneeling next to her. She blinked drowsily and stared deeply into his beautiful golden eyes. A sleepy smile of invitation curved her lips.

His eyes darkened, became molten gold. She breathed his name in a whisper of sound filled with longing. Reva lifted her hands, plunging her fingers into his dark blonde hair. The action seemed to ignite an inferno of desire in Chance. His arms locked around her, pressing her tightly against his muscular chest. And his mouth... have mercy, *his mouth.*

It took possession of hers. His kiss claimed her. *Owned her.* Demanded total capitulation which she willingly gave. It was a kiss like no other. Filled with heat and passion and a need that burned hot enough to incinerate. Her skin felt scorched, too sensitive for the clothes covering it. And her girly parts were on fire.

She mewled in protest when he tore his lips away from hers. The harsh rasp of his breath brushed her cheek and she forced eyes laden with desire open. The breath caught in her throat. Her hands had wreaked havoc with his hair, his face was flushed and his eyes burned hotly. But it was the fierce hunger in his eyes that mesmerized her.

Chance wanted her.

Well, of course, he did. This was *her* fantasy after all. It was *so* much better than the dreams she normally had about him. She caressed his cheek and was surprised to discover scratchy beard stubble. It felt amazingly real and his skin was as hot as if he were caught in the grip of a raging fever.

Both hands settled on his shoulders, slid slowly down his chest, learning the contours of his muscular body through the fine linen shirt. She felt his chest rise and fall with each harsh breath, the way his heart hammered against his ribcage. The shudder that shook him. As if he ached for her touch as much as she ached for his.

Reva lifted her eyes to meet his and sucked in a shocked breath. Because Chance looked like he was about to devour her. Hell yes! *Let the devouring begin.* "I want you," she said in a breathless voice that didn't even sound like hers.

"Thank God," he rasped in a guttural tone. A split second later, he rose with her in his arms and carried her into his office. Chance kicked the door closed and backed her against it. "You have no idea how much I want you, Ms. Blaine."

A frown knit her brow. He was not allowed to call her that in her dreams. It was too impersonal, and she planned to get very up close and personal with him. "Reva," she corrected indignantly because her dream lover should know that. "Call me Reva."

"Not now," he refused as his eyes ate her alive. "Ms. Blaine is the sex kitten that fuels my fantasies. You've teased me mercilessly with your curvy little body wrapped in prim and proper clothes. I've ached to let your hair down and wrap it around my wrist while I fuck you senseless from behind."

Her breathing hitched as shock filled her. *Have mercy!* This most assuredly was *not* one of her normal dreams. Because Chance didn't say things like that to her in them. Although it had been hotter than hell. Her fantasy life was definitely evolving into uncharted territory. And she liked it. *She liked it a lot.*

Her flaming cheeks must have given her away, because he laughed, such a wicked, *wicked* sound, and asked, "Did that shock you, Ms. Blaine? You have no idea the things I want to do to you. Did you know that when you blush it makes me want to strip you naked and fuck you until neither one of us can move?"

Her gasp became a moan of pleasure as his hands cupped both of her butt cheeks and squeezed. "This fine ass can make a man insane with need," he declared as he turned her around and slowly lowered the zipper on her pencil skirt.

Reva moaned and her thighs clenched together, surprising herself. Because she'd had no idea that having a man talk dirty to her could be so hot. Hey. Don't judge. It was *her* dream. She could be naughty if she wanted to. *Lord, did she want to.*

Her skirt slithered down her legs and she heard his ragged intake of breath. "Absolutely beautiful," Chance praised as he ran his warm palms over her bare cheeks. His fingers caught the center strap of her thong and tugged. The silky material abraded her sensitive clit and she flattened both hands against the door to remain upright.

She felt the pins being removed before her hair cascaded down to her waist. His fingertips massaged her scalp tenderly before trailing down the length of her mane. "So soft and silky," he said in a tone so seductive that she shivered. He wrapped the length around his wrist and tugged her head back. "Perfect, just like the rest of you."

Reva was practically panting in anticipation of what he would do next. Using her hair, he turned her to face him. She melted back against the door, eyes wide and hands splayed against it for support.

Because the man staring back at her was not her easy-going boss. Nor was he her fantasy lover.

This man was a sex god.

From the intensity of his gaze, it looked like he was going to make her his love slave. Oh, yes, please, she silently begged and couldn't imagine a better fate. Her heart hammered like a wild thing because Chance had never wanted her this desperately before. Not in *any* of her dreams. And she'd had some *really* good dreams about him.

He released her hair and began to unbutton her blouse. One, achingly slow button at a time. Reva would have happily ripped the darn thing off, but he seemed to be savoring the moment. Her heart was racing by the time he slid it from her shoulders. She watched his eyes darken even more as they locked onto her breasts.

Her eyes slid closed and a moan escaped her lips as he cupped them in his hands. Her knees began to tremble when his thumbs traced the edge of the lace cups, barely grazing her overheated flesh. "Gorgeous," he breathed in a raspy tone and placed a kiss on each one.

Have mercy. What this man did to her was downright sinful. She was ready for his complete and total possession and he'd barely touched her. Reva had never wanted anyone as much as she wanted Chance.

He gathered her hair in his hand and pulled it over one shoulder, draping it over her breast the way he wanted it. She opened her eyes and saw that he had taken several steps back and was just standing there staring at her intently. Like she was a work of art on display for his viewing pleasure.

She shivered in response to his heated gaze. Gooseflesh rose every place it touched. The man really was a sex god. He'd worked her into a frenzied state and all he was doing was looking at her. Lord help her when he finally got around to touching. She was definitely ready for the touching.

"I knew you'd look like this," he said in an awestruck voice. "Fuck me shoes and sexy lingerie. You've got a naughty side that you keep hidden under that straight-laced exterior, don't you Ms. Blaine?"

Reva couldn't answer him to save her life. Not that she knew what to say. Before this crazy dream, she would have said no, but now... she just didn't know anymore. Obviously Chance hadn't expected an answer because he moved toward her like a predator stalking prey. She didn't know how much more of this sensual torture she could take.

Bare inches separated them when he lifted his hand and trailed one fingertip over her plump bottom lip. "I fantasize about your mouth," he admitted in a sensually drugging tone. "Every time you peer at me over the top of your reading glasses I want to see you do it with my dick in your mouth."

The naughty words whispered over her and she shuddered in reaction. Reva felt her juices gush in response and she moaned raggedly. Her knees turned to mush and she swayed on her four-inch heels. Strong hands steadied her, guided her away from the door, across the room to his massive desk. Dazed with desire, she blindly followed.

He stood behind her and unclasped her bra. It fell away and his hands cupped her breasts, massaging, kneading before he tweaked her nipples. She stared at his tanned hands against her paler skin as a shudder shook her from head to toe. His hands slid up her torso, over her shoulders, down her arms.

He placed her palms flat on top of his desk, causing her to bend at the waist. Those masterful hands trailed up her arms and down her back, both soothing and exciting her fevered flesh. He circled the globes of her butt once, twice, before ridding her of the thong. His hands glided down and eased her thighs further apart.

"Fucking perfect," he breathed hoarsely.

She could only imagine how she looked with her butt in the air, legs spread wide, thighs damp with her own desire, breasts dangling freely. Reva looked back over her shoulder and saw that his eyes had a glazed, hungry look that matched his predatory expression. Chance was looking at her like she was a feast he was about to devour.

Have mercy, she wanted to be devoured.

One hand lightly caressed her right butt cheek while the other slid between her thighs. "You're drenched for me," he said in satisfaction. "Do you want me, Ms. Blaine?"

Beyond words, she licked her lips and nodded confirmation. She mewled in surprise when his hand connected against her butt cheek with a light smack. "Tell me," he commanded as he leaned over her and gently bit her neck.

"I..." the word came out raspily and she swallowed hard. "I want you."

"Yes," the word was a hiss of approval as he grasped her hair and wrapped it around his wrist. "I've wanted this since the moment I met you."

"God, yes," she panted and pushed her hips back against him. Chance met her thrust with his own. His dick slid partway in and she moaned her pleasure. His other hand grasped her hip and held her in place as he thrust home. Her back arched in response, her nails raked across the smooth polished wood.

He filled her completely, thrust after life altering thrust. Reva chanted his name like a mantra, begged and pleaded for more like a mindless creature. Her toes curled in her shoes, her legs were quivering like she'd run a triathlon. Heart hammering, chest heaving, she screamed his name like a wild banshee.

Fireworks exploded inside her body, sparks flowed through her extremities and burst out of her pores. Tears slid down her cheeks unnoticed as he thrust balls deep and cried her name brokenly. When Chance released her hair, Reva collapsed atop the desk, spent and boneless. She barely noticed when he lifted her into his arms.

He carried her over to the sofa, sat down and stretched them both out. His hands stroked her tenderly, soothingly as she floated slowly back to earth. A sated sleepy smile curved her lips and she uttered the only word that she could articulate, "Wow."

Chance laughed, the sound so deliciously wicked. "Wow is right," he agreed and placed a tender kiss atop her head. "You're mine now, Reva Blaine. I'm never gonna let you go."

"Mmm," she purred in utter contentment and came awake slowly. It had only been a dream. A beautiful dream that would never happen. Not to someone like her. But the fingertips lightly caressing her cheek felt very real, the touch so warm and gentle. A sigh of pleasure escaped her parted lips.

Reva opened her eyes, lifted her head and saw Chance kneeling next to her. She blinked drowsily and stared deeply into his beautiful golden eyes. A sleepy smile of invitation curved her lips. His eyes darkened, became molten gold.

Have mercy. *It was just like the dream!*

EPILOGUE

When a sleepy smile of invitation curved her lips Chance's heart skipped a beat. It damn near stopped when she breathed his name in a whisper of sound filled with longing. Reva plunged her fingers into his hair, igniting an inferno of desire in him. *Because his little sex kitten wanted him.* His arms locked around her, pressing her body tightly against his chest.

His mouth took possession of hers with the intention of claiming her. *Owning her.* He demanded total capitulation which she willingly gave. It was a kiss like no other. Filled with heat and passion and a need that burned hot enough to incinerate. His skin felt scorched, his heart was hammering wildly and his dick was too sensitive for the clothes covering it.

Chance knew he had to stop while he still could.

Or he'd take her right there on the desk.

He tore his lips away from hers and she mewled in protest. The sound inflamed him even more and it took every ounce of his self-control to keep from doing it again. A harsh rasp burst from his lungs when eyes laden with desire met his. Reva seemed mesmerized by the fierce hunger burning in his eyes.

But it was the desire in her eyes that damn near did him in.

She caressed his cheek before both of her hands settled on his shoulders, slid slowly down his chest, learning the contours of his body. A shudder shook his entire frame. He had ached for her touch for so long, and now that her hands were finally on him, his heart hammered against his ribcage so hard that he had to fight for each breath.

Reva lifted her eyes to meet his and sucked in a shocked breath. Chance guessed it was because she had just realized that he wanted to devour her. "This isn't a dream, is it?" She asked in a breathless tone that sent shivers down his spine.

"No," he rasped in a guttural tone.

A frown knit her brow. "You really want me? She asked and looked as confused as she sounded.

"You have no idea how much I want you," he replied as his eyes ate her alive. "You're a walking wet dream who's teased me mercilessly with your curvy little body wrapped in prim and proper clothes. I've been in love with you since we met, Reva. If you don't feel the same, for God's sake, walk away now."

His heart stuttered when she pulled out of his arms, but instead of moving away, she reached for her glasses. Reva slid them on her pert little nose, tilted her head down and peered at him over the top of them as if she knew it made him crazy. His dick swelled to epic proportions and every drop of blood in his head rushed south.

"I love you, Chance. I always have," she said in a breathy voice that would put a phone sex operator to shame.

His heart damn near exploded.

"You're mine now, Ms. Blaine," he said triumphantly as he scooped her into his arms. "My very own sex kitten."

"Mmm," she purred in utter contentment. "Yes, please."

The End

TONYA BROOKS

SHE'S MAKING ME

Crazy

I BOINKED THE BOSS SERIES

SHE'S MAKING ME CRAZY
Previously published as That Crazy Woman
I Boinked The Boss Series

TONYA BROOKS

CHAPTER ONE

"So, what did you think?" Liz Barlow asked in amusement since her employer's mouth was twisted in a frown.

"I think it will be impossible to replace you," Tyrell Canfield complained petulantly.

His personal assistant of five years was getting married and moving halfway across the country. He'd done everything he could to talk her into staying and hadn't had an ounce of success. Liz was convinced that she was in love, which meant she wasn't willing to be reasonable or rational, no matter what he offered as an incentive. Hell, he'd offered her everything *except* a marriage proposal, and if he thought that would work, he might consider it.

Losing her was going to be a nightmare. She handled his professional and personal life with practiced ease and so effortlessly that he never had to worry about anything. It would take a hell of a woman to fill Liz's shoes, and he was beginning to doubt he'd ever find someone. He'd been interviewing possible replacements all week and wasn't happy with any of them.

***

Liz laughed lightly at his pouty little boy expression. In spite of the fact that he was spoiled rotten when it came to women, her boss was an absolute teddy bear and she loved him dearly. She really hoped he had enough sense to appreciate the gift she was about to hand him on a silver platter.

"Well, I saved the best for last," she admitted and dropped a file on his desk. "This one is perfect for you."

"You think so?" He asked doubtfully and flipped open the personnel file. Since he preferred to promote from within the company, the human resource department had sent him every employee they had that was even remotely qualified for the position. But Liz had intentionally kept this applicant for last.

"I know so," she admitted smugly. Her roommate would be the perfect replacement for her position as well as the perfect woman for her boss. She'd shake up his regimented life and give him a real challenge. If there was one thing the notorious playboy loved, it was a challenge. When he raised one eyebrow at her tone, she asked, "Have I ever let you down, Ty?"

***

"Not until you decided to get married and live happily ever after," he grumbled and began to read through the file. Both eyebrows rose as he read. This applicant's credentials were very impressive and the letter of recommendation from her current boss was as well. Stanley Kemper was one of his top people and a man whose opinion he valued. It would seem he thought highly of his assistant. Very highly indeed. "So, why does she want a change?" He asked curiously.

"CJ really needs the additional income, otherwise she'd never consider leaving Stan. They work well together," she informed him seriously.

"So it seems," he nodded thoughtfully as he read through her file noting the many citations of praise she'd received as well as the regular salary increases. "You think she's the one?" He asked hopefully. Liz knew the job better than anyone. If she thought the woman could do it, it was practically a done deal.

"So will you," she assured him.

"All right. Send her in," he agreed in relief and leaned back comfortably in his chair as she went to get the last applicant. He flipped the file closed, convinced that this was the one he'd been looking for. Now he didn't have to worry about having his well-ordered existence turned upside down. *Hallelujah.* When the woman entered his office, Ty shot straight up in the chair as all the blood in his head migrated south.

Sweet Mother of God!

He had *not* been prepared for this.

The first thing he noticed was her legs. Long, gorgeous legs emphasized by the sexy as hell fuck me shoes. Legs that went on forever, he realized as his stunned gaze slowly traveled up the length of them. The skirt was pencil thin, stopping just below the knee, sliding sensuously across her thighs as she moved.

The suit coat was tailored, showing off every luscious curve, the lapels peeking open to reveal a tantalizing scrap of silk in the same shade of peacock blue as the suit. A mane of ash blonde hair hung loosely in a tousled style that looked as if she had just crawled out of her lover's bed. Those too kissable lips were set in a polite smile, and her eyes were the most amazing shade of silvery blue.

She was absolutely breathtaking.

And he had a hard as granite boner to prove it.

His PA had been right about one thing. She *was* perfect for him. This was the kind of woman he normally dated, the kind of woman he'd love to peel that suit off and explore every delicious inch of. The kind of woman he wanted in his bed. Unfortunately, this was *not* the kind of woman that he needed to stare at every day and not be able to touch.

Liz had lost her goddamn mind!

***

CJ Brooks had heard all about Tyrell Canfield and his womanizing ways from her roommate. Liz swore that he was a great guy, and an excellent boss, even if he did go through women faster than spit could disappear under a Texas sun. Liz also rationalized that when a man looked that good, he could afford to be picky.

CJ was *not* that charitable.

She had no use for a manwhore and was already prejudiced against him before they ever met. Tyrell Canfield obviously had no respect for the women he dated and discarded, and that type of behavior was inexcusable. In her opinion, he wasn't worth the lead it would take to put him six feet under.

She had seen him in the building on several occasions, and Liz was right. He *was* ridiculously handsome. It ought to be illegal, or a sin, or something equally dire for a man to be that attractive. But it took a lot more than a pretty face and a muscular body to make CJ lose her head. Their first meeting did absolutely nothing to change her mind.

When she stepped into his office, she could almost feel the heat from his brown velvet eyes as they traveled up her body. Good God. She was here for a job interview and he had practically undressed her with a look! She had to fight the urge to cover herself and her hackles rose in response. Typical manwhore. He couldn't even look at a woman and see her as anything except a potential bedmate.

The fact that she really needed this job was the only thing that prevented her from turning around and walking right back out the door without a word. Suck it up, buttercup, she instructed herself sternly as she stopped in front of the desk. When he just sat there staring at her with a peculiar expression on his too-handsome face, she extended her hand and said evenly, "Thank you for seeing me, Mr. Canfield."

***

God, she was perfect.

Absolutely perfect. Right down to the whiskey smooth and slightly smoky voice tinged with a soft southern drawl. Ty blinked as if coming out of a daze and hastily rose to his feet. He took her much smaller hand in his and felt a jolt of raw hunger surge through his veins at the contact. His boner happily bumped its own greeting against his zipper and he hoped like hell his suit coat was providing some coverage for the unruly appendage.

"Have a seat," he offered, his own voice a bit on the husky side as he forced himself to release her hand and sit. She sat gracefully across from him, shoulders straight, hands in her lap and ankles delicately crossed. Her expression remained neutral as she met his gaze with a level look. "Tell me about yourself," he invited, more interested in the woman than he had a right to be.

"What would you like to know, Mr. Canfield?" She inquired.

"Start with where you got that accent," he decided and flashed the panty dropping smile that women didn't seem to be able to resist.

***

All but mesmerized by that dangerously seductive smile, her nipples tightened in response and her body suddenly felt overheated. It was no wonder he had women fighting over him. The man was positively lethal. If he could get this kind of response with just a smile, she would melt into a puddle of goo at his feet if he ever touched her.

The hell she would!

CJ absolutely refused to be attracted to the odious man, regardless of how foolishly her body responded. She blinked once, careful not to let her expression alter in the slightest and answered evenly, "Texas."

***

"I thought so," he nodded as his smile grew even more dazzling. Odd how it didn't seem to have the slightest effect on her. Ty wondered why. The obvious reason would be a husband, but his eyes raked over her hand and didn't see a ring. "Married?" He queried and noticed her eyes looked completely silver now. He could have sworn they were bluer before.

***

Oh, he did *not* just go there, she thought indignantly. Her marital status had absolutely nothing to do with her ability to fill the position and he knew it. The insufferable ass had better not try to turn this interview into something personal. "No, sir."

"Engaged?"

Yep. He went there all right. Mr. Love 'em and leave 'em had better check himself real quick. There was no way in hell that she would ever become a notch on his intricately carved bedpost. You've got the wrong woman, bucko. With her dander up, it took a bit of effort to respond with a mild, "No, Sir."

"Seeing anyone seriously?"

That did it. CJ was outraged at the blatantly personal questions. She blinked and barely managed to stop a scathing response from slipping past her lips. If she didn't need this job desperately, she'd love to go all crazy bitch on the arrogant jerk and put him in his place. Why the hell had she let Liz talk her into this?

***

When she merely blinked at him instead of responding, Ty added, "I only ask because my current personal assistant is leaving to get married. I'd hate to find myself in that predicament again anytime soon." Not to mention the Human Resource department would raise holy hell if they knew he was asking this line of questions, to begin with. He was violating all types of labor laws at the moment.

***

Well, shoot. He had a darn good point, CJ realized. The situation did make those questions completely valid, and it made a lot more sense than thinking that he was interested in her. The man dated models and heiresses for God's sake. Now she just felt foolish and was thankful that she hadn't opened her mouth and ruined her chance at the position.

"That won't be an issue, Mr. Canfield," she assured him calmly. CJ didn't have time to date. The chances of her quitting to get married were slim to none.

***

"Excellent," he said in satisfaction, more than pleased that she wasn't already taken. Ty frowned inwardly and quickly squelched that line of thought. He had a firm rule against mixing business with pleasure and had never even considered dating an employee before. Finding a woman to share his bed was almost too easy to accomplish, but finding a good assistant had proven to be much more difficult.

There was no way in hell he'd jeopardize that.

Besides, having her complain to HR that he'd been hitting on her was a headache he did not need. Ignoring the fact that she was a beautiful woman was damn near impossible, but he gave it a try and liked what he saw. Her demeanor was very polished, completely professional, and she hadn't shown an ounce of interest in him.

Which was excellent.

But... she was just too damn attractive for his own peace of mind. Ty would much rather have a personal relationship with her as opposed to a professional one. However, her bland expression revealed that she was about as interested in him as she was in a hydro colonic cleanse, so this just might work.

If she put a bag over her head.

And gained a couple hundred pounds overnight.

Yeah, he was so screwed.

"Would you be willing to dress a bit less... attractively?" He asked on impulse. When those silver eyes merely blinked at him again, he felt compelled to add, "A beautiful woman in my office is a distraction that I neither want nor need."

***

The backhanded compliment did not impress her in the least. CJ was practically fuming at the absurd request. Why, the arrogant bastard! How dare he presume that she would intentionally dress to try to attract his attention? However, her expression and voice never altered as she assured him, "I'm certain that can be arranged, Mr. Canfield."

He smiled and looked genuinely relieved. "In that case, I'll see you Monday morning, Ms..."

"Brooks. CJ Brooks."

"What does CJ stand for?" Ty asked curiously.

She hesitated before replying, "Cassie Jo." It wouldn't have done any good not to tell him. It was in the personnel file laying on his desk. If the insufferable man had even bothered to read it, he would have known.

Ty rose and extended his hand. "Welcome aboard, Cassie."

She rose as well, gave his hand a firm shake and said coolly, "I prefer CJ."

"I don't." That charming smile daring her to contradict him.

She merely nodded cordially, "As you wish, Mr. Canfield."

***

"How did it go?" Liz asked hopefully when her roommate stepped out of her bosses office. She noticed the flashing silver eyes and sighed. "What happened?" CJ's eyes always turned silver when she was angry.

"I start Monday," she said flatly.

"But?" Came the wary response.

"He wants me to dress less attractively," CJ practically growled.

That was good and bad, Liz realized. It was good because it meant that Ty was interested and bad because CJ was obviously pissed. However, her roommate's anger did not overly concern her because there wasn't a woman alive who could resist Ty when he turned on that lethal charm.

In spite of his playboy reputation, he was a good man. Exactly the kind of man that CJ needed. And he'd never find a better woman than her friend. Even so, it was going to be an epic battle of wills before they came to the same realization. She'd be willing to bet her engagement ring on it. "And?"

Her lips parted in a smile that could only be described as devious. "I'm going to give the man exactly what he asked for," CJ assured her. "Before I'm through teaching him a lesson that he'd never forget, Tyrell Canfield won't know what hit him."

Liz smiled triumphantly and replied, "Let the games begin."

CHAPTER TWO

"Good morning, Ty," Liz said cheerfully when he walked in Monday morning.

"Morning. Where's Cassie?" He asked as he looked around the office.

Cassie? She barely bit back a laugh. He was *really* asking for trouble calling her that. "CJ is going over today's schedule with Stan's temp. I didn't think you'd mind since her transfer didn't allow him any time to choose a replacement."

"That's fine. Send her in when she gets back. And send Michelle dark pink roses," he requested.

"Am I going to have to guard your door this time?" Liz asked knowingly as she jotted down a note to call the florist.

Ty was a creature of habit who despised chaos in any form, especially when it came to his dating habits. It was a highly publicized fact that when he was dating a woman, he always sent her coral roses. When he was through with her, he sent dark pink roses, jokingly referred to by the media as the kiss of death.

Liz couldn't count the number of times that distraught women had called the office after receiving the pink roses. Quite a few of them had actually shown up in tears, and several of them had been after his blood. Dealing with the fallout was part of her job and it was never pretty. CJ would absolutely hate it.

***

"Doubt it," he denied confidently and went into his office.

Michelle wouldn't be showing up at his door or trying to entice him back. The woman was astute if nothing else, and she had realized this weekend that their time together was over. The fact that he had dropped her off at her place after the theater on Friday might have given her a clue that his interest was waning. When he canceled dinner Saturday for a night out with the boys, it was over and they both knew it.

Like everyone else, she would assume that he was moving on to the next woman who had caught his eye. Ty wished that were the case. The woman that he wanted was off limits, but that didn't seem to matter. He hadn't been able to get Cassie out of his mind all weekend and he'd almost managed to convince himself that she wasn't nearly as beautiful as he remembered.

Truth be told, he'd been anxious to see her this morning and find out if he was just deluding himself. Now he was going to have to come up with a reason for having her come to his office. Maybe he could offer to let her spend some time with Stan's temp every morning. Yeah, that would work. Hell, any excuse would do as long as he could see her again.

"You wanted to see me, Mr. Canfield?" Cassie inquired as she entered his office.

Surprised because she had voiced his thoughts aloud, he looked up and his jaw dropped in shock. She was wearing a pair of sensible black flats, a voluminous black skirt that hung just above her ankles, and a black blazer that completely hid her shape. Her glorious hair was pulled back in some kind of clip and a pair of god-awful tortoise shell glasses were perched on her nose.

Gone was the beautiful woman he'd been fantasizing about all weekend and in her place was a somber, dour looking creature that he had no desire to look at. "What the hell have you done to yourself?" He demanded incredulously.

"You instructed me to dress in a less attractive manner, Mr. Canfield," she reminded him and he could have sworn her lips twitched in amusement.

His mouth dropped open again before he snapped it shut. "I didn't mean for you to look like an old maid," he protested and was appalled that she'd taken him this literally. Frustrated because she didn't look like she should, *like he wanted her to*, he snapped, "I find black depressing. Don't wear it again."

"As you wish, Mr. Canfield," Cassie agreed blandly.

"And for God's sake let your hair down," he all but growled.

Without a word, she reached up to remove the clip and her hair cascaded over her shoulders like a silken cloud. "Anything else, Mr. Canfield?" She inquired pleasantly.

Jesus. The simple act of letting her hair down had been blatantly erotic, and the boner had gone on red alert. Ty wanted to see her do that while she was naked. *Preferably astride him.* He had to swallow twice before he could speak. "Feel free to help the temp out until Stan chooses your replacement."

***

"Certainly, Mr. Canfield," CJ replied and walked back out into the outer office wearing a smug expression.

"Well?" Liz asked a bit anxiously and hoped her friend's little demonstration didn't ruin her plans to hook the pair up.

"He's learning," she grinned.

CHAPTER THREE

Tuesday morning, Ty entered the office and smiled cheerfully. "Good morning, ladies," he greeted and was pleased to see Cassie's hair looking all tousled and sexy like it should be, and she was dressed in beige.

"Morning, Ty."

"Good morning, Mr. Canfield."

"Cassie, can I see you in my office when you have a moment?" He inquired pleasantly, and she rose to follow him. He sat down at his desk, took a good look at her and frowned. Damn, this wasn't a bit better. The beige suit was just as shapeless as the black one had been and she was still wearing those ridiculous shoes. She slid the glasses on and the frown became a scowl. "Do you wear contacts, Cassie?"

"No, Sir."

"Could you?" He asked hopefully. Those tortoise shell things really were hideous, and they hid her gorgeous silvery blue eyes.

"I don't need them, Mr. Canfield," she admitted evenly. "The glasses are just to make me less attractive, as you requested."

He bit back a curse and drummed his fingers on top of the desk impatiently. "Perhaps I was a bit... remiss in requesting you do so," he decided. "I find I prefer a more... youthful appearance."

"Youthful," she repeated as if she wasn't quite certain of his meaning.

Deciding that it would be better to be precise instead of vague this time, he suggested, "Something more form fitting. And shorter skirts. *Much* shorter."

***

CJ actually went so far as to write his specifications on the notepad she had brought in with her. "Form fitting, shorter, more attractive, youthful clothing," she reiterated. "Anything else?"

"Get rid of those shoes," he commanded. "Wear something with heels."

"Certainly, Mr. Canfield," she agreed blandly and added that to the list. Oh, the man just didn't know when to quit. Teaching him not to be an arrogant ass was going to be too much fun.

CHAPTER FOUR

Ty walked into the office Wednesday morning and nearly had a stroke. His new personal assistant was wearing a pair of strappy stilettos with a miniskirt so short that it was probably illegal in the Bible Belt. The sweater that clung to her like a second skin plunged daringly low in front, offering his stunned gaze a perfect view of her ample cleavage.

Needless to say, the boner was back to stay.

"Cassie!" He exclaimed in shock at her attire and in awe of the curvaceous body it revealed.

"Good morning, Mr. Canfield," she said evenly.

"What the hell are you wearing?" He choked out.

"Exactly what you requested, Sir," she said evenly and turned to reach for her notepad.

When his assistant bent over her desk, the miniskirt rode up to reveal that those long gorgeous legs went right up to her... *Sweet Mother of God!* She was wearing a red thong and his boner damn near erupted at the sight.

She turned to face him while reading the notes aloud. "You specifically requested I wear form-fitting, shorter, more attractive, youthful clothing, with heels."

Ty had just come to the realization that the crazy woman didn't have an ounce of common sense. *And that she was too damn sexy for her own good.* God, she looked magnificent in the outfit even if it was entirely inappropriate. "My office," he growled when he could speak. "Now."

"Is something wrong, Mr. Canfield?" She inquired pleasantly, a puzzled look on her beautiful face as she entered the office behind him.

He rounded his desk to keep a safe distance between them. At this point, he didn't dare get close enough to touch her. If he did, he'd have her laid out across his desk while he sank balls deep inside her. The boner thumped its approval of that idea. "You look like you're going to a nightclub," he snapped and raked a hand through his hair in agitation.

She pulled at the hem of the skirt as if she were uncomfortable with it. "It certainly isn't *my* idea of office apparel, but I was trying to conform to your wishes as best I could, Mr. Canfield," she pointed out.

The sight of those gorgeous legs was making it hard to think. *And breathe*. Especially with his heart beating like a wild thing and the damn boner threatening to burst through his pants. Ty dropped wearily into the desk chair and commanded, "Just dress like you did the day I interviewed you."

"As you wish, Mr. Canfield," she agreed blandly but he could have sworn he saw her lips twitch in amusement.

CHAPTER FIVE

Thursday morning, Ty was prepared for the worst when he walked in the office, but the sight of his new personal assistant dressed in the same lovely suit she'd worn the previous week filled him with a deep sense of satisfaction. Now, *this* was how she was supposed to look. Classic beauty with sexy undertones.

She was perfect again. *Thank God.*

"Good morning, ladies," he greeted cheerfully. "Nice suit, Cassie."

"Thank you, Mr. Canfield," she said evenly, but her smile was positively mischievous.

***

That evening, the two of them wound up in an elevator alone together. Ty took the opportunity to appreciate what a truly beautiful woman she was as he asked, "Are you settling in comfortably, Cassie?"

"Yes, Mr. Canfield," she agreed. "I hope my performance has been satisfactory so far."

He could find no fault with her work. The woman was as efficient as she was beautiful. It was a shame she didn't have a damn bit of common sense. Then again, she'd only been trying to please him. Ty wondered if she'd be as eager to please him in bed. Annnd, just like that, the boner was back.

"Yes. Quite satisfactory," he agreed huskily.

The elevator came to a jarring stop, the lights went out, and they were left unexpectedly in the dark. A split second later, the emergency lights came on and his personal assistant had plastered herself against him, her eyes huge, round blue orbs of sheer terror. Oh, hell. Just what he needed. A panicking woman.

"It's all right, Cassie. I'm right here with you," Ty said soothingly and very reluctantly peeled her too enticing body off of his. Yeah, there was no way in hell that holding her would end well. Being caught having sex in an elevator was *not* on his bucket list. The boner forcefully thumped its disagreement.

Stupid appendage.

"The power will be back on in a minute," he assured her and fervently hoped it was. Those glazed eyes fixed on him, but he wasn't sure she was really seeing him. Her breathing was shallow, her pulse was racing and her pupils had dilated. At least she wasn't screaming. At that unpleasant thought, he decided to keep talking and keep her as calm as possible.

"Why don't we sit down and get comfortable?" Ty suggested and gently lowered them both to the floor. This wasn't the first time he'd been stuck in an elevator so he removed his suit coat and tie, loosened the buttons at the neck of his shirt and smiled reassuringly at her. "Let me take your coat off. It'll get warm in here in a few minutes and this will keep you cooler."

He slid the coat off of her shoulders and groaned at what he revealed. She was wearing a silky camisole and apparently nothing else beneath it. Her nipples were jutting forcefully against the soft material, the outline of her breasts easily discernible even in the dim light. He'd love nothing better than to tease those hardened peaks into aching buds with his tongue.

Flames of fire licked up his spine at the thought. Jesus, an ice bath wouldn't be able to cool him down if he didn't get his mind off of getting her naked. Forcing his eyes back to her face, he said confidently, "It's going to be fine, Cassie. These things happen all the time."

He took her hand in his and she clenched it like a lifeline. Ty was surprised at the strength of her grip. Her hands were slender and delicately molded, her fingers long and elegant. God, how he'd love to feel those hands on his body, stroking his heated flesh, wrapped around his... He bit off the thought with a muttered curse and sweat beaded his brow.

The electricity came on just long enough for the car to jolt abruptly before they were plunged into total darkness. Cassie cried out in fear and launched herself at him, knocking him backward onto the floor. She climbed on top of him as if she were trying to get inside his skin. Her arms wrapped around his neck, her breathing rough and ragged, she clung to him with a death grip.

White hot heat slammed through him and his arms closed instinctively around her trembling body. "Cassie, it's all right," he crooned, his hands as soothing as his tone as they caressed her back. "I'm here. I've got you."

The car jolted again, the emergency lights came on, and she whimpered in fear, burying her face in his shoulder, her legs locking around his as she pressed herself even closer. Her pelvis was pressed so tightly against his boner that he could feel her heat. Dear God, she was killing him by degrees. Ty wanted her so much he could barely breathe.

Rolling so that she was beneath him, he stared down at her beautiful face. The tear filled eyes tore at his heart and clawed unmercifully at his conscience. Lowering his head, his lips covered hers tenderly, gently, offering nothing more than solace. Before he was sure how it had happened, Cassie had taken control of the kiss. Her arms slid down his back to press his chest closer to hers, her mouth claiming his with a voracious need that sent him completely over the edge.

Ty landed in a pool of pure scalding desire as he deepened the kiss even more, his mouth feasting on hers ravenous with need, his hands caressing anything he could reach. He heard her moan softly, felt her body arch up against him, her legs tighten around his, her pelvis rocking against him and he lost all sense of reason.

***

CJ was in pretty much the same condition. She'd known that she would melt into a puddle at his feet if he ever touched her and damned if she hadn't been right. God, the sensations coursing through her were too incredible to believe. The whole thing was almost surreal.

The floor beneath them seemed to shudder and shake much as her body was doing and then she felt weightless as if she were sinking deeper and deeper into this wonderful madness. On some level, she was vaguely aware of the sound of bells. Soft, ting-ting sounds. *Holy moly.* Ty's kiss made her hear bells ringing!

***

"You folks all right?" The amused maintenance worker questioned as he stared down at them when the doors opened.

Ty lifted his head and was surprised to discover that not only had the elevator started working again, but it had carried them to the lobby without him being aware of it moving. Damn! That was one hell of a kiss. He could only imagine what having sex with her would be like. The thought boggled the mind.

"Yes," he replied hoarsely as he rose up on his knees and lifted Cassie up into a sitting position. They stood a bit shakily and stared at each other for a long tense moment before she broke the spell and looked away.

***

CJ grabbed her purse and coat with hands that shook and hurried out of the elevator. She stuffed her arms into the sleeves as she crossed the lobby, her cheeks flaming with mortification. Good God. It was bad enough that she'd had a full blown panic attack, thanks to that damned claustrophobia, but she could not believe that she'd practically molested her boss. And on the elevator floor for heaven's sake! She didn't even want to know what *he* must think of her behavior.

***

Ty was thinking it was too incredible to believe and he couldn't wait to pick up where they had left off. He caught up with her on the sidewalk and slid his arm around her waist.

"Mr. Canfield, please," Cassie protested as she pulled away from his loose embrace.

His smile was truly wicked when he responded, "Sweetheart, after that kiss I think you should call me Ty."

"I'll do no such thing," she refused, heat rushing to her cheeks. "You're my boss and I don't..."

"You just did," he interrupted in amusement.

"Well, I can assure you it won't happen again," she said firmly and waved frantically at a taxi driver to get his attention.

"Why the hell not?" He frowned.

"I don't sleep with my boss, Mr. Canfield," she said coldly and stepped into the cab, slamming the door closed behind her.

CHAPTER SIX

Friday morning, a very disgruntled Tyrell entered his assistant's office and grunted at Liz when she greeted him. "Where is she?"

"Stan's office," she said and looked surprised at his tone.

"Send her to me," he growled and went into his office to pace the floor.

Ty was not pleased with the way things had ended the night before. He'd gone home alone, again. Slept alone, again. Suffered through the most incredibly erotic dreams about Cassie, *again*. The woman had become a damned obsession, and he didn't like it. He'd been celibate since he'd met her because *she* was the only woman he wanted.

The only woman he *couldn't have*.

But last night had changed things. Now he knew what she tasted like. How her body felt beneath his. *How hot her passion burned.* Jesus, another few minutes and they would have gone up in flames. She had hidden it well, but now he knew that she wanted him too. It was time to let this attraction run its course.

He'd deal with the fallout later. She could always go back to working for Stan, at her current rate of pay, of course. Ty knew he would have to go through the whole interview process again, but damn it would be worth it. To have her in his bed was worth any price he had to pay. He wanted Cassie, and he wasn't taking no for an answer.

When she entered his office a few minutes later, that damn bland expression on her face, he wanted to kiss her senseless. He wanted the passionate woman he'd held the night before, not the unemotional PA that stood before him. "About last night..."

"I spoke to the maintenance supervisor this morning," she interrupted briskly. "He assured me it was just a power failure and not a malfunction. It shouldn't happen again, Mr. Canfield."

He fixed her with a hard stare. "That wasn't what I was referring to," Ty said silkily. When she merely stared back at him with that damn look, he added, "And you know it." She didn't bother to argue, so he took that as a positive sign. "I have tickets to the theater tonight, Cassie, and I'm in need of a beautiful woman to accompany me."

"Certainly, Mr. Canfield," she agreed.

The easy acquiescence surprised and pleased him. It would seem that his assistant had had a change of heart about dating her boss. *Thank God.* "I'll send a car to..."

"Perhaps it would be simpler to meet at the theater," she suggested.

He lifted one brow but didn't bother to argue the point. They might arrive separately, but she was going home with him. For damn sure. His boner thumped its approval with enthusiasm. Ty gave her the address and time of the show and she queried, "Would it be all right if I left a little early today?"

Assuming that she wanted extra time to dress for their date, he readily agreed, "Take all the time you need." Ty grinned wickedly when she went back to her office. This was going to be a night to remember. It looked like his dry spell was coming to an end. Celibacy really sucked.

***

That evening, Ty stood in front of the theater and glanced at his watch impatiently. Where the hell was she? Cassie was always punctual. A frown knitted his brow. If she stood him up, he'd wring her gorgeous neck. *After* he covered it with kisses.

"Mr. Canfield?"

"Yes," he admitted warily as he looked the woman before him over from head to toe.

"*Tyrell* Canfield?" She asked with a wicked smile as she returned the inspection.

"Yes," he responded a bit more hesitantly, wondering how the hell a prostitute knew his name. There was no doubt of her profession. She was wearing a black leather micro miniskirt, black lace-up thigh-high boots and a hot pink sequined halter top with a glow in the dark lime green marabou scarf.

"Hot damn," she said in approval. "The service didn't tell me you were gorgeous."

"Service?" He repeated in confusion.

"Little Vixens Escort service," she clarified.

"I beg your pardon?" He responded and had no idea what she was talking about.

"I'm your date for the evening, honey," she said with a wicked laugh.

"My..." *Sonuvabitch!* Cassie wouldn't dare. She couldn't have... but he knew it was true. The crazy woman had hired him an escort! *He was going to kill her.* Slowly. With his bare hands. "I don't need a... date," he managed to say evenly.

She placed her hands on her hips, her heavily made-up face becoming annoyed as she demanded, "Why the hell not?"

"Someone made a mistake," he said firmly. Yeah, his PA had made a mistake all right. She just didn't know how big of a mistake it was yet. But she would. When he got his hands on her...

"Now look, Canfield," the woman said angrily. "I got all dressed up, had my nails done and everything."

Ty glanced at the curious faces around them uncomfortably since she'd raised her voice enough to be overheard. "Look, Miss..."

"Nirvana," she supplied.

"Nirvana," he said with a groan. Ty really was going to kill Cassie for this. "I'm sorry if you've been inconvenienced, but..."

"Inconvenienced?" She expostulated in a shrill tone as she glared at him and poked a sparkly purple claw-like fingernail in his chest. "I went to a hell of a lot of trouble for this, buster. Cab fare alone cost me a damn fortune, so if you think for one minute... take your hands off me!"

Ty had taken her by the arm and was leading her away from the entrance of the theater since the woman insisted on making a spectacle of herself in public, but he released her immediately and hissed, "Keep your voice down. I'll pay for the cab fare. Hell, I'll pay for the evening if that's what it takes. Just go away."

Somewhat placated at getting paid for her trouble, she folded her arms over her obscenely large breast implants and pouted, "And I really wanted to see this show."

"You can have the ticket," he offered in complete disgust and pulled them out of his pocket. "Here. Take both of them."

"Really?" She asked in surprise and then threw her arms around him and kissed his cheek with a loud smacking noise. "Thanks, Mr. Canfield. You're a prince."

A prince, he scowled furiously as she teetered precariously toward the theater on five-inch heels with his much-coveted tickets. Sucker was more like it. But the one responsible for ruining his evening was about to get her goose cooked.

Ty stalked back to his car, grabbed his iPad and connected to his office computer via the cloud. He quickly pulled up the personnel files and got Cassie's home address. He tossed the iPad in the passenger seat and cranked the car. When he arrived, he recognized that this was the same building that Liz lived in. Recalling the address, he realized it was the same apartment.

The women were roommates.

Well, that was too damn bad. Liz would just get to see him chew her friend out, and unless he changed his mind, he might chew on his former personal assistant as well. Liz had to know the woman that she had suggested as her replacement was a raving lunatic. Ty slammed the car door and went up to the third floor with fire in his eyes.

"Ty!" Liz said in surprise when she opened the door. "What a wonderful surprise. Come on in."

It was obvious that they were having a party, and he recognized several of his employees inside. So much for the ass chewing plan. Some things were best unpublicized. Like how his new PA had deliberately made a fool of him. "Hello, Liz," he greeted evenly as he stepped inside the apartment.

"Good evening, Mr. Canfield," Cassie said cordially as she joined them. "So glad you could make it to Liz's surprise going away party."

"Surprise is right," Liz laughed as she hugged her roommate. "Apparently CJ's been planning this for weeks and I never even had a clue. It was so sweet of you to let her leave early today to get everything set up before I got home."

"Cassie is very good at surprising people it seems," he said with a pointed look.

"Are you on your way to the theater?" Liz asked since the woman knew his schedule better than he did.

"My... date didn't turn out like I'd planned," he said dryly and could have sworn he saw Cassie's lips twitch before her expression became bland again. "So, I decided to stop by and wish you well."

Liz hugged him. "That's so sweet, Ty," she said sincerely. "Come on in and mingle."

"I can't stay," he refused and even managed a smile as he kissed her cheek. "Have a good life, Liz."

"Thanks, Ty," she said and squeezed his hand.

"Cassie, I'll see you Monday," he warned and left.

***

In spite of his ominous tone, CJ couldn't help laughing when she closed the door behind him. She had known that Ty would be furious, but it wasn't like he could fire her for refusing to date him. Liz kept saying that the man's well-ordered existence needed to be shaken up, and she was just the woman to make it happen.

CHAPTER SEVEN

Ty was not a happy man when he walked into his office Monday morning. He'd had the entire weekend to stew over Cassie's joke and he'd wavered between her being insane or just plain malicious. Either way, he wasn't about to let it happen again. The fact that she looked incredible didn't deter him in the least.

His first impulse was to kiss her senseless and then chew her out. He quickly decided that it would be more prudent to chew her out and *then* kiss her. At least that way he'd get around to it. If he touched her, he wouldn't think about anything except getting inside her. The boner was in complete agreement.

He stalked across the room, placed his palms flat on her desk and leaned forward menacingly to growl, "What the hell were you thinking?"

"I beg your pardon?" She asked evenly, the silvery blue eyes meeting his.

"What possessed you to hire me an escort?" He demanded bluntly.

Her brow furrowed in confusion. "But I was only doing what you asked me to, Mr. Canfield."

His expression was incredulous as he exclaimed, *"What?"*

"You said you had theater tickets and needed a beautiful woman to accompany you," Cassie reminded him.

"And you thought that meant I wanted you to hire an escort?" Ty demanded and really wanted to put his hands around her slender neck and squeeze.

"What else could you have meant?" She asked innocently, her eyes huge and uncertain. When his mouth dropped open, she asked somewhat hesitantly, "Was she not to your liking, Mr. Canfield? I specifically told the receptionist that she had to be beautiful."

He rose and stalked around the desk as he snarled, "I meant for *you* to accompany me."

"Me?" She gasped in surprise. "Mr. Canfield, I told you I wouldn't date my boss."

"Fine," he snapped. "For future reference, I'm perfectly capable of finding my own woman without the aid of a service. Is that clear?"

"Certainly, Mr. Canfield," Cassie agreed. When he started toward his office, she asked, "Was the theater business or pleasure?"

"What damn difference does it make?"

She held up an invoice. "The service emailed me the bill. If its business, I'll send it down to bookkeeping for processing."

He made a strange gurgling sound deep in his throat. God Almighty! The last thing he wanted was for people to think he'd hired an *escort*! He snatched the invoice out of her hand, snarled, "I'll handle it," and stalked into his office, the door slamming behind him.

***

CJ sat there grinning cheerfully and a moment later heard him roar, *"Six hundred dollars!"* She buried her face in her hands to hide the sound of her laughter.

CHAPTER EIGHT

Ty lost count of the times that he was sorely tempted to fire the crazy woman over the next few weeks. But damn, she really was good at her job. Just as efficient as Liz, if not more so. Cassie anticipated his every need in advance and had an uncanny ability to know exactly what he wanted before he did.

Except when it came to her.

God, he wanted her more every time he looked at her, and he spent *a lot* of time looking at her. She had him so tied up in knots that he didn't know if he was coming or going most of the time. The fact that she seemed completely immune to him only served to frustrate him even more. Cassie acted as if the kiss in the elevator had never happened.

Just the thought of that kiss made him break out in a cold sweat. It had been hard enough not to see her as a desirable woman before. Now it was damned impossible. Ty walked around with a boner constantly and no relief in sight since no other woman but Cassie could satisfy the need that she had caused. It was slowly driving him out of his mind.

She was so beautiful that just looking at her could take his breath away. He wanted her so much that being near her made him ache in ways he didn't understand. But being away from her on weekends was sheer torture. He craved her presence in ways he couldn't even conceive. He was obsessed and something had to give or he was going to lose it.

Ty decided that he needed to get her out of the office and make her forget that he was her boss. She needed to see him as a man. A man who was desperate for her company. Her touch. Her all-consuming passion. He'd come up with a way to mix just enough business in with pleasure to get her to comply, and he hoped like hell the idea worked.

"I'll be entertaining some prospective clients Friday night, Cassie. I need you to arrange a dinner party and accompany me," he informed her. When she merely blinked at him, he added firmly, "It's business." No way in hell did he want another escort fiasco to happen.

She nodded her agreement. "How many people?"

"James Colton and his wife."

"From Texas?" She queried.

"That's the one," he agreed. "I've been talking with him for months and he's finally agreed to have an informal meeting. This has to be perfect, Cassie. He's got several other offers as well and they're going to be wined and dined the whole week they're here. Our dinner party has to be over the top, so spare no expense."

"Certainly, Mr. Canfield," she agreed. "Perhaps we should host it at your home."

"Why?" He asked in surprise.

"Texans are friendly and sociable. We like to get to know the people we deal with personally," she explained. "Interacting with you in your home and getting to know *you* will play a large role in his decision. I can almost guarantee everyone else will take him to a restaurant."

That was exactly what he wanted to do with *her*. If it worked with James Colton as well that was just an added benefit. Not to mention having her at his place would make seducing her so much easier after the guests left. Hell, he couldn't have planned it better himself. "All right," he agreed cheerfully. "Do whatever you think is best."

***

CJ went back to her office wearing what she was sure was a sappy smile. Liz had been right. Ty really was a great boss. He was so laid back and easy going that he was a joy to work for. At least he was when she wasn't trying to teach him a lesson which she had done on more than one occasion.

When she wasn't trying to antagonize him, he was always cheerful, quick to offer praise, and he pretty much let her do things the way she wanted to without interference. The man was just so darn likable that it made it hard to recall why she had disliked him so much in the first place.

Not once had he requested she send those loathsome roses to a single woman, nor had she fielded phone calls from the women that he had dumped. She hadn't even seen his picture in the paper with the flavor of the week on his arm.

If she didn't know better, CJ could almost believe that he wasn't the same man that her roommate had worked for. The Tyrell Canfield that she knew was sweet and considerate and nothing like the manwhore she had believed him to be. He was the kind of man that she could lose her heart to.

Every day it became harder and harder to maintain the facade of disinterest.

Her foolish heart skipped a beat when he walked into a room. Her girlie parts clenched in anticipation when he flashed that mesmerizing smile. *And that kiss!* Oh God, she would *never* forget that kiss. CJ had never really known how all-consuming desire could be, but she did now.

It was a constant battle not to give in to his devastating charm. The only thing that stopped her from jumping his gorgeous body was the fact that he was her boss. A relationship with Ty would not last and she simply could not afford to lose her job.

CHAPTER NINE

Friday evening, Ty walked into his penthouse and the first thing he noticed was the mouth-watering aroma of food. The second thing was the unmistakable sound of a steel guitar. Then he noticed the wall filled with floor to ceiling windows that offered a dramatic view of the skyline had changed drastically.

He stared incredulously at the rooftop terrace where bales of hay were stacked on top of each other at random intervals and a live band was tuning up at the far end of the pool. A long line of tables piled high with food flanked one side, their checkered tablecloths flapping in the breeze.

"Everything is ready, Mr. Canfield," Cassie smiled as she met him at the Arcadia doors.

"What the hell have you done?" He asked in a strangled tone. This was *not* what he'd had in mind at all. The Colton's would think he'd lost his damn mind. The crazy woman was going to cost him the contract. He just knew it.

"Arranged a real Texas-style barbecue," she informed him cheerfully.

"A what?" He choked.

Cassie gestured to what looked like a regular backyard grill jacked up on steroids where the carcass of a large animal was being roasted. "A barbecue," she repeated.

Ty closed his eyes in frustrated fury. Why the hell had he trusted her with something this important? He knew she didn't have an ounce of common sense and this proved it. "Cassie, I'm going to kill you," he breathed.

"But, Mr. Canfield, the Coltons will love it," she said and seemed to be genuinely surprised at his reaction.

"You've turned my terrace into a... a... *barn!*" He accused as he looked around again.

"Hay is biodegradable, so if any of it blows away, it won't hurt the environment," Cassie assured him.

He made a strange gurgling sound at the thought of hay drifting through Manhattan and snapped, "I'm surprised you didn't put sawdust on the floor."

"I thought about it," she admitted. "But I was afraid it would clog up the pool filters."

The fact that she was serious pushed him completely over the edge. Ty really was going to kill her. It would be justifiable homicide. The crazy woman was single-handedly ruining his life and his business. No court in the world would blame him. The worst they could do was put him in a nut house.

Because she was making him crazy!

He grasped her shoulders, intent on at least shaking some sense into her, but once he had his hands on her, that idea dissolved in a wave of heat. Ty hauled her against himself and kissed her senseless. When Cassie stared up at him in bemusement and whispered, "Ty," white hot heat surged through him and he crushed her against his body, his mouth claiming hers with a desperation he didn't even try to hide.

***

Bells, she thought dreamily. I hear bells every time he kisses me. "Excuse me, Ms. Brooks," she vaguely heard an amused voice say. When Ty reluctantly lifted his head, she turned a dazed look on one of the catering staff. "Hmm?" CJ asked without any real concern.

"The doorbell is ringing," the young woman informed her.

"Thank you," she smiled in that delicious desire laden haze and looked back at Ty again. And that's when she realized what she was doing and *who* she was doing it with. "Oh hell," she breathed in horrified disbelief, pulling her arms from around his neck and hastily taking a step back.

***

"I'll get the door," Ty said in resignation and went to greet his guests. *With a damn boner.* "Mr. Colton, it's good to finally meet you."

"Call me Jim," the big man offered as he shook his hand. "This pretty little filly is my wife, Selena."

"What is that heavenly aroma?" Selena asked with a stunning smile as she shook hands with him.

"We're uh, having a... barbecue," Ty said lamely.

Jim's face lit up. "Best news I've had all week," he grinned and slapped Ty on the back in approval.

"It was my, um, assistants idea," Ty admitted in shock and genuine relief.

"If it tastes as good as it smells, she deserves a raise," Selena suggested. "We were just talking about how good a barbecue sounded after all the fancy food that we've been stuck with this week."

"I thought you might," a soft feminine voice said as Cassie joined them. "So I arranged for a little slice of Southern hospitality right here in downtown Manhattan."

Before Ty could make the introductions, Jim Colton boomed, "CJ!" and snatched Cassie off of her feet and into a bear hug. Realizing that his potential client seemed to know his assistant came as quite a surprise. A wave of sheer possessiveness washed over him and the urge to punch the other man out was as shocking as it was unexpected.

Jim laughed in delight as he put Cassie back on her feet. "Good lord, darlin', you're all grown up."

"Considering I was fifteen the last time you saw me I should hope so," she laughed when he released her.

Jim introduced her to his wife and said, "I've known this young'un since she was in diapers. CJ's daddy is the best wildcatter I ever knew. How is old Jake?"

The smile faded and the joy in those big silvery eyes turned blue as she said, "He had a stroke a few years ago, Big Jim. His left side is paralyzed."

Genuine regret showed in his expression. "I'm sorry to hear that, CJ," Jim assured her. "It must be hard for a man like Jake being tied down like that."

"He makes up for it by terrorizing the nurses," she assured him with a faint smile.

"Nurses?" He frowned.

The blue eyes darkened even more. "I had to put him in an assisted living facility so he'd have constant care," Cassie said heavily. "I tried keeping him with me at first, but he kept trying to do things he wasn't able to. After he set the kitchen on fire, I didn't have any other choice."

Jim nodded his agreement. "I'd like to visit him before we leave," he suggested.

The smile brightened again. "You'd be good medicine," she agreed.

"Where is he?" He asked, and she told him the name of the facility. "I'll go by tomorrow."

"I'll see you there," she agreed. "I spend every weekend with him. The nurses appreciate the break."

"No doubt," he laughed.

"Well, what do you say we move on out to the patio and try that barbecue?" Cassie suggested.

"Wonderful idea," Selena readily agreed.

Once Ty realized that Jim was just an old friend of the family, his ire quickly calmed. Hearing about her father came as another shock and in that unguarded moment, he had seen the guilt and pain in her expression. Cassie was obviously carrying a heavy emotional burden because she wasn't able to care for her father herself.

From what little he knew, those full care facilities were expensive, and he decided right then and there to look more deeply into the matter. There was no way in hell he'd allow her to scrimp and barely make ends meet while she worked for him.

Hell, he'd pay for her father's care himself if he thought she'd let him. Somehow he didn't think that idea would go over well. He'd be willing to bet that her pride would never allow such a thing. But there were ways around that.

Cassie didn't know it yet, but she was going to be getting a substantial raise very soon. Having a parent entirely dependent on her had to be difficult, and if Ty could help ease that burden financially then that's what he would do. He just wished she'd open up and let him ease the emotional burden as well.

The thought jerked him sideways.

Had he just considered having an actual relationship with Cassie? The kind that came with emotions and sharing and all the other entanglements that he had skillfully avoided all these years? Damn right he was. If that was what it took to have her by his side and in his bed where she belonged. Because no matter how hard he fought it, he knew that they were meant to be together.

Now he just had to convince her.

The evening went perfectly. The food was excellent, the music was incredible, and the Coltons were relaxed and happy. Ty wanted to kiss Cassie for her brilliance. The crazy woman might have scared him half to death, but she'd known exactly what she was doing. All in all, the evening was a complete success and he couldn't imagine how it could have been any better.

Well, there was one thing that would do it, and the sooner he got her in his bed, the better. But first, he had to get her back in his arms. As soon as their guests left, he suggested, "Dance with me."

"Mr. Canfield..."

"After all the hard work you put into this, the least you deserve is to enjoy a dance," he insisted and pulled her into his arms. "Why didn't you tell me you knew the Colton's?"

***

"I wasn't sure Big Jim would remember me," she admitted and tried not to enjoy the feel of being in his arms. Talk about a losing battle. There was no place that she would rather be and being this close to him was the sweetest form of torture.

"Tonight was perfect. You did a hell of a job, Cassie," Ty assured her.

"Thank you, Mr. Canfield."

"I thought you'd lost your mind when I saw all of this," he confessed. "How did you come up with the idea?"

"I know what it's like to be away from home and miss the things that make it home," she said in a wistful tone that she wasn't aware of. "Thank you for letting me have the barbecue. I enjoyed it as much as they did."

"So did I," he admitted. "I can't remember the last time I ate that much."

"The caterers are excellent," CJ agreed. "I found them once when I was looking for some really good barbecue for Daddy. He gets so sick of the bland food they feed him at the facility."

"Then you'll have to take him some of this," he offered.

"Thank you, Mr. Canfield. I'd already planned to," she grinned.

"Are you ever going to call me anything but Mr. Canfield, Cassie?" He asked hopefully.

"Not as long as you're my boss," she denied when the song ended and she stepped away. "Good night, Mr. Canfield."

CHAPTER TEN

The next morning, CJ arrived at the assisted living facility and the first thing her father asked was, "Is that barbecue I smell?"

"Your favorite," she agreed indulgently and kissed his cheek.

"Pumpkin, you're an angel," Jake Brooks sighed happily once he'd eaten.

"Feel like another surprise from home?" She teased when she saw Jim at the door.

"Like what?"

***

"Like me you old reprobate," Jim grinned as he walked into the room.

"Big Jim," Jake laughed in delight. "What the hell are you doin' in these parts?"

"Just doin' some business," he replied as they shook hands. "I ran into CJ last night and when I found out you were here, I had to come see how you were doing."

"Glad you came," he agreed.

"I'll leave you two to swap lies about the good old days," CJ said as she headed for the door.

"She grew up real nice, Jake," Jim complimented.

"Yeah," he scowled. "Never thought she'd be takin' care of me."

"Listen, Jake, if you need anything, and I mean anything, you just let me know," his guest said seriously.

"Thanks, Jim. I appreciate it," he nodded. "But the only thing I need is for that gal to find a good man and settle down."

"That shouldn't be too hard," Jim grinned. "CJ's a real beauty."

Her father snorted at that. "She's not likely to find herself a man when she insists on spendin' every weekend here with me," he complained. "Hell, she don't even date."

"She doesn't?" He asked in surprise.

"CJ ain't the kind of woman to put up with no smooth talkin' city dude," Jake grumbled. "Now if we were back home, I don't doubt some young buck would have swept her off of her feet by now."

"So you need to get her back to Texas," he suggested.

Jake shook his head regretfully. "These dang homes are expensive as hell. She's got a real good job makin' more money than she could at home. I've tried to talk her into going back, but it's a wasted effort."

"You know I always need people in my organization. I'm sure we could find her a position and at the same salary," Jim offered.

"You'd do that?" The older man asked in surprise.

Jim squeezed his shoulder affectionately. "Jake, there ain't much I wouldn't do for you and you know it."

"I suppose we could mention it to her and see what she says," he nodded.

"I suppose we could," the younger man grinned.

***

To say that CJ was shocked was an understatement. Jim's offer nearly floored her. Taking her father back to his beloved Texas was a dream come true, or at least it had been until she'd met Tyrell Canfield. For some dang foolish reason, the thought of leaving him was unbearable. "Can I think about it?" She hedged.

"Take all the time you need," Jim agreed.

CHAPTER ELEVEN

Friday afternoon, Cassie stuck her head in his office to say, "You have a visitor, Mr. Canfield."

"Who is it?" He asked a bit irritably. His mood had soured the minute he'd walked in that morning. It was a beautiful summer day and Cassie had chosen to wear a dress that showed off every curve to perfection and emphasized those gorgeous silvery blue eyes. Frustration could make a man cranky as hell, he discovered.

"Surprise," an all too familiar voice said cheerfully, and he looked up to see a petite silver-haired woman standing in the doorway grinning happily at him. "Mom!" Ty exclaimed in shock as he shot to his feet. "What are you doing here?"

"Visiting you, dear," she laughed as he moved around the desk to hug her. She grasped his face in both hands and pulled him down to kiss his cheek.

"This is a surprise," he admitted and wasn't altogether pleased with it. He loved his mother dearly, *in small doses*. For such a tiny little thing, she had a will of iron and was a human dynamo when she set her mind to something. Her current project was to find him a wife and nothing he said or did deterred her in the least.

"Isn't it?" She laughed and seemed delighted that she had managed to surprise him. "I couldn't have done it without CJ's help. Such a lovely young woman. You're so lucky to have her, Ty."

"What did she do?" He questioned in confusion.

"I called earlier in the week and you were in a meeting," she explained. "Dear CJ chatted with me for a while and when I mentioned that I'd love to come for a visit, she offered to make all the arrangements. Isn't she just wonderful?"

The look he gave his personal assistant promised dire retribution. "Wonderful," he said from between clenched teeth that passed for a smile.

"I know you're busy, so I won't keep you," Eleanor said and patted his hand. "CJ hired a car to drive me around while I'm here and the driver is the dearest thing. He's going to take me on a tour of the city."

"Great. Have fun, Mom," he encouraged and wondered if the driver charged by the mile or the hour. "I'll call the doorman and ..."

She waved her hand airily. "No need. I told you, CJ handled *everything*. They're expecting me."

"Great," he said from between clenched teeth again.

"Oh, I almost forgot. CJ made our reservations for dinner, so don't be late," she warned.

"Wouldn't dream of it," he denied. Great. Just fucking great. Now his personal assistant was screwing up his personal life even more. "Cassie, when you've shown my mother out, I need a word."

"Certainly, Mr. Canfield," she agreed and followed his mother into the outer office.

"Did Tyrell call you Cassie?" He heard his mother ask before the door closed. "Such a lovely name."

***

"Thank you, Mrs. Canfield. I was named after my mother."

"Do you mind if I ask what the J stands for?" She inquired.

"Not at all. Cassandra Josephine is the proper name, but everyone called my mother Cassie Jo."

"I'll bet she's just as lovely as you are," the older woman smiled warmly.

"She died when I was born, so my father named me after her," CJ explained. "It broke his heart to call me Cassie, so daddy just called me CJ."

"How tragic," Eleanor sighed and patted her hand in genuine sympathy. "Is your father still with us?"

"Yes, Ma'am, although his health isn't what it was," she confessed, and the sadness shown in the blue eyes.

"I'm so sorry, my dear," Eleanor said sympathetically. "I lost my own dear husband when Ty was a boy. I'm afraid I spoiled him terribly after that."

***

"It must have been hard raising him alone," she sympathized. "My father wasn't quite sure what to do with me in my teenage years."

"He did a wonderful job," the older woman smiled. "You're a lovely young woman."

"Thank you, Mrs. Canfield."

"Now, you must call me Eleanor," she insisted. "I just know we're going to be dear friends."

CJ gave her a genuine smile. "I'd like that Eleanor," she agreed and impulsively added, "And you may call me anything you like."

Her smile brightened even more. "You should join us for dinner tonight."

"Oh, I couldn't possibly," she demurred.

"Of course you can," she overruled. "Ty will probably be bored out of his mind listening to me prattle on. It'll be nice to have a woman to chat with."

"I'd love to, but I'm afraid I have a prior engagement," she apologized.

"Oh? Well, bring your young man along. He and Ty can entertain each other," she suggested.

That thought amused CJ so much that she agreed, "All right, Eleanor. We'll meet you there."

"Better yet, I'll send the car for you," she suggested with a sly wink. "After all, I might as well get Ty's money's worth."

***

"How dare you go behind my back and make arrangements for my mother to visit," Ty fumed the instant she stepped inside his office.

Her eyes widened in genuine surprise at the rebuke. CJ had not done it to bedevil him. On the contrary, she had genuinely wanted to do something nice for him for a change. "I beg your pardon?" She questioned with a frown.

"Under no circumstances are you to *ever* involve yourself in my personal life again. Is that clear?" He demanded.

"Quite clear, Mr. Canfield," she agreed in confusion. "I apologize for overstepping. I was merely trying to do something nice for you... your mother. She's a wonderful woman."

"She can also be a royal pain in the ass," he complained and was not looking forward to the barrage of prospective brides that he knew his mother was going to be parading before him. The last time she'd come for a visit, he'd been stuck entertaining every marriage-minded female in Manhattan he recalled and scowled in frustration. "How long is she staying?"

"Eleanor asked me not to book her on a return flight yet," she admitted. "She said she'd leave when she felt the need to do so."

Which meant that his mother wasn't planning to leave until she found him a fiancée. Like hell. There was no way that Ty was going to put up with that again. He glared at Cassie since this whole fiasco was her fault. "Since you arranged this mess, you'd damn well better be prepared to entertain her."

***

"I already have," she assured him and began to understand what his mother had meant about her last visit not being quite so pleasant. Her son obviously didn't want her there. "I arranged for the car so she could be independent, and I purchased tickets for several events that she'd like to attend. Eleanor was quite pleased with the itinerary."

"I ought to fire you for this," he fumed.

CJ lost her temper at his callous behavior, and since her job was already in jeopardy, she gave him a piece of her mind. "What you ought to be is ashamed of yourself," she accused as her eyes flashed silver. "Your mother is a wonderful woman, and she obviously adores you. Some of us... some of us aren't that lucky."

***

Ty had been surprised at the rebuke, but when her voice broke and he saw tears shimmering in those beautiful silvery blue eyes, he realized that he'd been behaving like a spoiled brat. "You're right," he admitted ruefully and managed a lopsided smile. "I'm sorry, Cassie. I love my mother dearly, but she…" He shook his head since there was no way to explain and said instead, "Thank you for being nice to her."

Having regained her composure, she replied in that bland voice, "No need to thank me, Mr. Canfield. I did it for Eleanor."

Which meant she hadn't done it for him, ungrateful bastard that he was, he deduced.

***

"You did what?" Ty asked that night when he got home.

"Invited Cassandra to join us for dinner," she repeated cheerfully.

Oh, hell. Here we go. "*Who* is Cassandra?" He asked warily.

"CJ."

A huge smile lit his face, and it was decidedly wicked. "You invited Cassie?" Yes! Now he had another chance at seducing her.

"Yes. She's bringing her young man along to keep you entertained."

"*Her what?*" He barked.

"Cassandra has a date, so I told her to bring him along," Eleanor explained.

So much for seduction, Ty thought grimly. Now he was going to be forced to watch Cassie make goo-goo eyes at another man. *Like hell.* He pulled the cell phone out of his pocket and began to scroll through the contacts.

***

"What are you doing?"

"Inviting a date to join us."

"No, Ty," his mother refused and took the phone away from him. It was obvious that her son was interested in his lovely assistant and nothing could have pleased her more.

"Mom," he complained.

"No, dear. I need an escort and you're it," she insisted and wasn't about to let him flaunt one of his floozies in front of Cassandra. "Now, go get dressed or we'll be late."

***

Ty did as he was told, muttering under his breath the whole time. By the time they arrived at the restaurant, he'd worked himself up into a fine temper. He had decided to just go ahead and punch the other man out when they met and have done with it.

"There's Cassandra," Eleanor enthused when she saw her. "Oh, and her young man is adorable."

Adorable. His own damn mother was conspiring against him.

"Good evening, Eleanor. Mr. Canfield. May I present Bobby Taylor," he heard Cassie's whiskey smooth voice make the introductions.

Ty turned in his seat and glared pure venom, but the only thing he saw was Cassie. The boner sprang to attention. God, she looked fabulous in a dress the same silvery blue as her eyes. His hungry gazed roved down the length of her as he rose and he was shocked to see a little boy standing next to her. *Cassie had a son?* Every male molecule he possessed roared a denial at the thought of her bearing another man's child.

*That should be **his** son!*

As that staggering revelation bounced around in his brain like a ping pong ball on acid, he was vaguely aware of his mother greeting the child. As if in slow motion, the boy turned his attention on Ty and grinned revealing a tooth was missing. "Hello, Mr. Canfield," he heard him say, and it sounded like he was underwater.

Ty sank slowly back into the chair, his hand automatically reaching out to shake the child's. "Bobby," he said hoarsely.

"Thank you for inviting us," the boy said politely and moved around the table to sit next to Eleanor in the chair the Matre'd pulled out for him.

"How did you come to be in the company of such a charming young man?" His mother inquired of Cassie and Ty mentally braced himself for a revelation that he was certain would destroy his sanity. *Or what was left of it.*

"Bobby's parents are celebrating their anniversary tonight, so he and I are keeping an eye on each other," she replied with a smile.

Relief washed over Ty and left him as limp as a wet blanket. The child wasn't hers. *But his would be.* Just as sure as God made little green apples, he knew that Cassie was going to be the mother of his children. Now he just had to convince her of that. His mood much improved, Ty decided to tease her a bit.

"Baby sitting on a Friday night, Cassie? I assumed you'd have a hot date."

"I don't have time for a personal life, Mr. Canfield," she said evenly.

That was about to change. Ty had every intention of their relationship becoming about as personal as it could get. For the rest of the evening, he was at his most charming and couldn't miss his mother's pleased expression. His behavior didn't seem to impress Cassie at all since that damn bland expression never left her face.

Determined to change that, he kept filling her glass with wine and by the end of the meal, she was slightly tipsy and had actually relaxed enough to give him a genuine smile. Should've got her drunk to begin with, he thought in regret and gave serious thought to spiking the office water cooler.

"Dinner was lovely," Eleanor smiled tiredly. "I don't know when I've enjoyed myself more."

"Then we should do this more often," Ty announced, more than happy for an excuse to spend time with his beautiful PA outside of the office.

"An excellent suggestion," his mother readily agreed. "However, I'm simply worn out and ready for bed."

So much for doing this again, dammit. He couldn't take his mother home *and* seduce Cassie. "The night is young, Mom," he wheedled. "How long has it been since you've been dancing?"

"Too long," she laughed and patted his hand. "But not tonight, dear. Perhaps Cassandra would like to go dancing."

Now she was talking, he thought in triumph.

"Oh, I can't," Cassie denied. "It's already past Bobby's bedtime."

Damn. Ty just couldn't catch a break. It was a pity he couldn't send his mom and the kid home in a cab and take Cassie dancing. God how he needed to hold her in his arms again.

"Ty, why don't you take CJ and Bobby home and I'll take the car," Eleanor suggested.

"The car?" He repeated blankly.

"I had my driver pick them up, so he'd be here to take me home in case you young people wanted to make a night of it."

Ty could have kissed her. "Excellent idea, Mom," he readily agreed and called for the check. The kid would fall asleep and then he could take advantage of being alone with Cassie. Perfect plan.

"I couldn't possibly impose, Mr. Canfield," Cassie refused. "Bobby and I can take a cab."

"Nonsense," he countered and wasn't about to let her wiggle out of it. "Besides, your date is about to fall asleep sitting up and he's too heavy for you to carry. I'll take you home, Cassie."

"Thank you, Mr. Canfield."

"Call me Ty," he offered and knew there was no way she could refuse with his mother sitting right there smiling happily at them.

"Thank you, Ty," she said softly and set his pulse racing.

Ty carried Bobby through the restaurant, put his mother into her car where she cheerfully waved goodbye. When his car was brought around, he placed the child in the back seat, secured the seatbelt around him and turned to help Cassie into the passenger seat. Ty tipped the valet, climbed behind the wheel and drove away wearing a satisfied smile.

When they reached her apartment, he assisted her out of the car and carried a sleeping Bobby upstairs to place him on the bed in Liz's old room. "Thank you for bringing us home, Mr. Canfield," Cassie said in dismissal as he followed her back into the living room.

"Ty," he corrected as he removed his coat and draped it over the back of a chair. The tie was long gone as he'd tossed it as soon as they had gotten in the car.

"I'd prefer to keep our relationship strictly professional," she insisted.

"I'd prefer to kiss you," he admitted as he advanced on her, a determined gleam in his eyes.

***

"Mr. Canfield, I don't date my employer," she reminded him as she backed away, more than a little unnerved by the look in his eyes. The look that said he was tired of waiting that he wanted her and intended to have her. The look that had her quaking in her knock-off designer shoes because she wanted the same damn thing.

"You're fired," he replied as if that solved everything.

CJ stopped when the back of her legs hit the front of the sofa and stared at him incredulously. "You'd fire me because I won't sleep with you?"

"So you will," he corrected and pulled her into his arms.

"You can't be serious," she protested.

***

"You have no idea how serious I am," he denied as he lowered his head and placed a kiss just below her ear. She shivered at the touch and he smiled against her silky skin. "I'll do whatever it takes, Cassie. Anything you want me to," he promised and trailed his lips down the curve of her neck as she moaned softly. "Just tell me what you want."

Cassie looked up into his eyes and barely breathed, "You."

That was the magic word. His mouth covered hers tenderly, but tenderness wasn't enough for either of them. They began to devour each other with voracious need, both of them clawing at the other, trying to get closer, always closer.

***

Bells, she thought dreamily. Every time this man kissed her, she heard bells.

"Cassie," Ty said as he placed nibbling kisses down her neck.

"Hmm?" She sighed.

"Are you expecting someone?"

"What?" She asked without concern and then gasped when he kissed a particularly sensitive spot below her ear.

"The doorbell. Someone's at the door."

"Someone's... oh!" She exclaimed and pulled away from him to hurry to the door. CJ was so frazzled that she didn't even use the peephole to see who it was. She opened the door and was surprised to see her neighbor standing there. "Robert."

"Hi, CJ," he grinned cheerfully as he walked in uninvited and stopped short when he saw Ty glaring at him in a most unwelcome manner. "Did Bobby behave?"

Bobby, she wondered in confusion and then realized what he meant. Good God, she had completely forgotten about Bobby! "Oh. He was an angel as always," she hastily assured him. "He fell asleep on the way home."

"I'll get him and get out of the way then," he said and went into the bedroom to scoop up his sleeping child. "Thanks again, CJ. I really appreciate it. Sandy and I haven't had a night out in months."

"Anytime, Robert," she smiled and closed the door behind him.

CJ turned around, fully prepared to send her boss packing. Then she saw Ty looking all mussed and rumpled and forgot every reason why she should send him away. His velvet eyes practically devoured her, but his expression lacked its usual confidence. He looked wary and uncertain, nothing like the arrogant manwhore she had once thought him to be. This man was simply irresistible, and she'd never wanted anything more.

***

Ty stood there staring at the woman watching him intently and bit back a curse. Here it comes, he thought in resignation. She's going to kick me out and go back to pretending like there's nothing between us. *Again.* He watched in disbelief as Cassie turned to the door and twisted the deadbolt before turning back around to face him.

His heart began to pound like a wild thing.

The boner did a tap dance in his pants.

"Cassie?" He asked hopefully, cautiously. Without a word, she walked slowly toward him, took his hand and led him to her bedroom.

***

CJ was trembling from head to toe in a combination of nervousness and anticipation. This was insane, and she knew it. The problem was that she just didn't care anymore. She was tired of fighting the attraction. Tired of trying to convince herself that she didn't want him. This had been inevitable from the moment they met and they both knew it.

She stopped beside the bed, released his hand and looked at him over her shoulder. The lamp she had left lit on the nightstand cast a soft glow over the room and the hunger in his eyes was plain to see. "Can you unzip me, Ty?" She asked in a voice that she barely recognized.

***

The sound of his name in that whiskey smooth voice trembling with need filled a place deep inside his soul. Ty trailed his fingertips up the side of her arms and across her shoulders to the center of her back. He slid the zipper down in slow, measured increments, his lips pressing tender kisses along her spine as he uncovered it.

She turned to face him as the dress slid to the floor and revealed a body he'd only seen in his wildest dreams. Not even his imagination could have conjured up anything this perfect. The breath froze in his lungs. The boner gave his navel a fist bump. His heart felt like it was going to explode.

***

CJ reached back, unfastened her bra and tossed it aside. Her thumbs hooked in the sides of the matching thong and slid it over her hips. She stepped out of her shoes and looked up to see Ty staring at her as if he'd never seen a naked woman before.

Emboldened by his reaction, she arched one brow and said crisply, "I believe you're overdressed for the occasion, Mr. Canfield."

The overly efficient personal assistant tone snapped him out of the trance and his eyes narrowed in warning. "What did you call me?"

"Mr. Canfield," CJ replied mischievously and then squealed in surprise when he lifted her up and tossed her onto the bed. Laughing in delight at his playfulness, she swung the hair out of her face and saw him removing his shirt. She drank in the sight of his broad shoulders, well-defined chest, and *holy moly* those abs!

Lord, the man was ripped more than her favorite jeans.

***

Ty pounced on top of her, linked his fingers with hers and placed their joined hands on the pillow beside her head. He gave her a mock scowl and growled, "Say my name."

Her lips twitched before her expression became bland and Cassie replied, "Mr. Can..."

His mouth claimed hers in a kiss ravenous with need until they were both breathless. Ty lifted his head and stared down at her bemused expression in satisfaction. "Say it, Cassie."

"Ty," she sighed.

"I don't ever want to hear you call me Mr. Canfield again," he said in satisfaction. "Am I making myself clear, sweetheart?"

"Just shut up and kiss me," she demanded and arched her body up against his.

His mama did not raise a fool.

Ty kissed her as if his life depended on it. The boner was convinced that it did. But he had waited too long to rush this. Their first time together had to be an unforgettable experience. Cassie was like a fine wine and he was going to savor every touch, every taste until he knew each nuance of her passion.

He took his time and caressed her gorgeous body as she writhed beneath him. When his fingertips brushed over a particularly sensitive spot, she tried to wriggle away. A devilish smile curved his lips as he tickled her while she shrieked with laughter. He'd never seen her look so carefree and happy before and Ty promised himself that he would fill her life with love and laughter.

While she was still smiling up at him, he kissed her as reverently as if she were the rarest and precious gift he'd ever received. And she was. Cassie had stolen his heart just as easily as she had wreaked havoc with his well-ordered life. She might drive him crazy on occasion, but he could not imagine his life without her.

CHAPTER TWELVE

Ty woke with the dawn and stared down at the beautiful woman curled against his side. God, he wanted to wake her up and make love to her again. In spite of the incredible night they'd shared, he needed her more now than he had before he'd touched her. He hadn't known it was possible to want a woman this much. Hadn't known he could feel this connected to anyone, and the feeling was so right that he never wanted it to end.

Sliding silently from the bed, he dressed quietly in the semi-darkness and placed a tender kiss on her lips. Cassie sighed softly, a smile curving her lips, and it took everything he had to leave her. But he didn't have a choice. His mother would worry if he didn't come home.

Besides, it wouldn't do for her to know the extent of his relationship with his PA. Not when she was already harassing him to find a wife. That his mom adored Cassie was more than obvious. One hint that he was serious about her and Eleanor Canfield would be sending out wedding invitations before he had a chance to propose.

Not wanting to leave her without a word, Ty went into the living room and spotted a neatly organized desk. Rummaging through the drawers, he found a pad and pen and left her a note. Grinning happily, he let himself out and shut the door silently behind him.

***

CJ woke and her hand slid across the bed searching for Ty. When she discovered his side was empty, she opened her eyes, sat up and looked around. He was gone. Pain washed over her and she fell back against the mattress as tears filled her eyes. Fool, she silently accused. She'd known it would be a mistake to sleep with him and she'd been right.

He'd gotten what he wanted and disappeared.

Oh, God, what have I done?

Broken every promise that she'd ever made to her herself and the cardinal rule that she lived by. It was bad enough that she had slept with her boss, but she had compounded that mistake by falling in love with him. Not only had she jeopardized her job, she knew it would only result in a broken heart. *Again.*

But, oh God, it had been worth it.

To know the tenderness of his touch, the heat of his passion had been worth any price. She had known that Ty would be an incredible lover, but what had really surprised her had been his playfulness. They had laughed and teased each other before, during and after the most mind blowing sex imaginable. She sighed in a combination of satisfaction and regret.

Refusing to dwell on what couldn't be undone, she slid out of bed. There would be time enough to deal with the fallout on Monday. At that depressing thought, CJ took a long, hot shower and got dressed in a pair of jeans and a cotton top. She took the bus to the retirement home and entered her father's room with a tired smile.

"Good morning, Daddy."

***

"Pumpkin," Jake grinned happily. They had their usual conversation and caught up on the past week, but he noticed the sadness his daughter couldn't seem to hide. "Who is he?" He questioned bluntly.

"Who?"

"The man that took the sparkle out of your eyes," he clarified.

"No one important," she denied.

"Want me to shoot him?"

"Will you?" She asked with a hint of a smile.

"I still got one good arm," he assured her. Jake Brooks had been a bear of a man, strong, active and completely fearless. The stroke had done its damnedest to break his spirit, but there was still a lot of fight left in him. Especially if a man was playing with his daughter. "Tell me about him."

***

"He's arrogant, spoiled and too damn handsome for his own good," CJ complained as she got up and stared out the window.

"The man's gotta have some redeeming qualities."

"What makes you think so?"

"Cause you're in love with him," he deduced.

"For all the good it'll do me," she grumbled. "He's not the type of man to settle down, Daddy."

"How do you know?"

"Because he's my boss."

Jake scowled and asked, "The dude who sends those kiss of death flowers?"

She laughed bitterly. "That would be him. Although I haven't sent his ladies flowers, Liz did it all the time." And then a horrible thought occurred to her. If Ty sent her those damn roses, she'd castrate him with a dull blade.

***

By Sunday night, Ty was bordering on frantic. He had wavered between fear and anger for most of the evening. He'd called Cassie repeatedly and kept getting the damn answering machine. Not knowing if she was there and avoiding him, he'd gone to her apartment that afternoon and demanded the manager let him in. She hadn't been home, and he had assumed she was still with her father.

He had checked her answering machine and discovered the damn thing was broken. Her mobile number hadn't been listed in the personnel file and he made a mental note to get it from her as soon as possible. Frustrated, he went back home and kept calling right up until eleven o'clock. She couldn't have stayed at the facility this long, could she? But where the hell else could she be? If she was with another man, he knew he wouldn't be able to handle it.

Cassie was his now.

There was no way in hell he was gonna let her go.

CHAPTER THIRTEEN

Monday morning, CJ arrived at work with a sense of dread. God, she hated having to face Ty again. When she got home last night, she had been shocked to discover that he had left her a note. In the bold handwriting that she had become so accustomed to, it read:

Cassie,

Have to go or Mom will worry. Wish I could stay. Will call later.

Ty

P/S - I kissed you goodbye.

Ty hadn't just snuck out like a thief in the night. Although the idea of a grown man leaving her bed so his mother wouldn't worry might sound like a load of cow pies to some, having met Eleanor, she knew it was true. CJ had witnessed firsthand how close the two of them were at dinner and thought it was adorable that he really did dote on his mother.

The answering machine's flashing red light had announced that there were twenty-seven missed calls, so she knew that Ty had called. *Repeatedly*. It was just as well that the thing was broken. She really didn't want to know what he might have said. Finding the note was enough to weaken her resolve that a repeat of Friday night could never happen again.

A wave of relief washed over her when she didn't see a vase of coral or, God forbid, pink roses on her desk as she'd half expected. Not that he could be bothered to order them himself, she thought uncharitably. If Ty even suggested that she send herself flowers, she really would castrate him.

The lone white rose lying in her chair came as a surprise and CJ picked it up with a hand that trembled. The gesture was so sweet and romantic and she couldn't believe that Ty had done this for her. She wondered how he had known that she loved white roses even as she assured herself that he had no idea what the flower signified. Two strong arms slid around her from behind and she froze in place.

***

"Good morning, sweetheart," Ty said huskily, his lips nibbling at her neck.

She whirled away from him protesting, "Mr. Canfield, please."

"Don't start that again," he warned as his hand lifted to caress her cheek.

"We happen to be at the office, Mr. Canfield," she reminded him as she quickly put the width of the desk between them. "You may not care what people think, but I certainly do."

So that was it. She didn't want the rest of the employees to know about them. Ty didn't have a problem with that. *For now.* "All right," he agreed easily, the wicked smile teasing his lips. "We'll do it your way."

***

It was almost five and Ty called her into his office to invite, "Have dinner with me."

"I don't think that would be appropriate, Mr. Canfield."

"You don't," he frowned. Ty rounded the desk and pulled her into his arms. "Then what would be appropriate?"

She pulled away from his loose embrace and said in that bland voice, "I don't date my boss, Mr. Canfield."

"Dammit, Cassie, don't start that again," he warned. "Friday night was..."

"A mistake," she interrupted. "One that will not happen again."

"The hell it won't," he countered.

"Mr. Canfield, please. This is difficult enough like it is," Cassie said heavily.

"You're the one making it difficult," he complained.

"I will *not* date a man I work for again. *I won't do it, dammit.*"

He was surprised at the vehemence he heard in her voice and it made him think long and hard before he commented gently, "I'm not the bastard who hurt you, Cassie."

"Maybe not," she agreed tremulously. "But I'm the same fool who'd wind up getting hurt."

Ty couldn't think of a single thing to say as he watched her turn and walk away.

CHAPTER FOURTEEN

The days dragged by and CJ was strung as tight as a rubber band. Every morning she found another perfect white rose waiting for her. The man was persistent, she'd give him that. He didn't say a thing to pressure her, but she felt his eyes on her constantly. Watching, always watching.

Like some patient hunter waiting for his prey to show an ounce of weakness before he moved in for the kill. Big Jim's offer was looking better by the minute. She didn't know how much more of this she could take. God, she wanted the man as much as she loved him and not being able to have him was killing her by degrees.

***

By Friday, Ty was at the end of his rope. He just didn't know what to do. Desperate for help, he went to visit the one person that he hoped could give him some insight into the situation. "Mr. Brooks, I'm Ty Canfield," he said as he stepped inside the room. "I'd like to talk to you about your daughter."

The older man paled visibly. "Is CJ all right?" He asked anxiously.

"She's fine," he hastily assured him. "I'm sorry, Sir. I didn't mean to alarm you."

***

"Thank God," Jake breathed in relief and frowned when the name registered. "Canfield. CJ works for you."

"And that's the problem," he grumbled.

The shrewd gray eyes didn't miss a thing. "Have a seat and tell me about it," he offered.

Ty sank down in the chair and said bluntly, "Mr. Brooks, I'm in love with your daughter."

"Is that a fact?" Jake asked in satisfaction.

Ty stood in agitation and began to pace. "The problem is that she won't take me seriously," he complained. "Hell, she won't even go out with me because I'm her boss."

"Sounds about right," he agreed.

The younger man stopped pacing and suggested, "Then maybe you can tell me why."

"I can," he admitted. "But you're not gonna like it."

***

"Somehow I don't doubt that," Ty said as he sat back down again. He didn't like knowing that another man had hurt Cassie, and the last thing he wanted was the details. But he needed to understand why she was so determined to avoid him so he could figure out how to change her mind.

"I blame myself more than anyone else," Jake admitted heavily. "You see, I used to be a wildcatter, and I had to go where the work was. That meant I had to leave CJ for weeks and sometimes months at a time. She was just eighteen and as trusting as a newborn babe when she got her first job. The man she worked for showered her with attention and she fell in love with him. The bastard seduced her and then threw her away like yesterday's paper," he growled angrily. "As if that wasn't bad enough, he filmed the whole thing and put it on the internet."

Ty's face showed the absolute fury that he felt. "I hope you killed him," he ground out harshly.

Jake gave him a level look and replied, "Let's just say he got what was coming to him," he agreed. "CJ moved out here where no one knew her, but she still doesn't trust a man not to hurt her again. Especially a man she works for. Or one known for changing women as often as his socks."

He nodded his understanding since his reputation was well deserved. "It looks like I've got my work cut out for me," he sighed.

"Well, don't drag your feet," Jake warned. "You might not have too much time left."

"What do you mean?"

"CJ's been offered another job, and she's considering it," he informed him.

"That might not be a bad idea," Ty nodded thoughtfully. "If she wasn't working for me, then she couldn't use that as an excuse."

The older man shook his head. "The job's in Texas."

"Texas?" Ty barked in surprise as he stood and began to pace again. "She can't move to Texas," he said more to himself than the other man. "Dammit, I can't lose her."

"Like I said, don't drag your feet," Jake reiterated. "My daughter is as stubborn as she is beautiful."

"What can I do to make her trust me, Mr. Brooks?"

"Had the same problem with her mama," he admitted with a grin of remembrance. "Damn stubborn woman just would not believe I wanted to settle down and marry her."

That got his attention. "What did you do?"

"I took her to an abandoned line shack and made love to her until she agreed to marry me," he admitted with a wicked smile. "Then I told her father what I'd done. He would've skinned me alive if she hadn't married me."

Ty couldn't prevent a smile at that. "There aren't many line shacks in Manhattan," he pointed out in amusement.

"I used what I had. Be creative," the older man suggested.

"I don't think it would have the same effect," he denied. "Cassie probably wouldn't buy you skinning me alive."

The look he gave the younger man was as hard as glass. "I can still use a shotgun and my daughter knows it," Jake assured him. "You'd do well not to forget it either."

It took a minute, but a smile of satisfaction covered Ty's face. "Mr. Brooks, I think we're gonna get along just fine."

The older man smiled as well. "Call me Jake, son."

***

Eleanor breezed into CJ's office and stopped short when she saw the vase of roses sitting on the credenza. "Oh, my!" She exclaimed in delight. "Someone loves you a great deal."

CJ turned slightly and saw the vase that she had placed behind her so she wouldn't have to look at the beautiful buds. "I wish that were true," she said softly.

"But of course it is, Cassandra," the older woman chided gently. "Don't you know the meaning of a white rose?"

"I do," she nodded. "But the person who sent them doesn't."

"That's a shame," she said regretfully. "My father was a botanist, you know. He taught me the meaning behind all types of flowers, but people don't take things like that into consideration anymore. They just send a particular flower because they think it's pretty."

Curiously, she couldn't help asking, "What does a coral rose mean, Eleanor?"

The older woman's smile turned into a frown since she obviously knew about her son's preferred flowers for his floozies. "Coral represents desire. And just so you'll know, dark pink means thank you."

CJ's lips turned down in a frown as well. "That figures." Leave it to Ty to send the perfect color even if he didn't know what it meant.

"Do you mind if I ask who sent the roses?" She asked hopefully.

"Do you mind if I don't answer?" Came the equally hopeful response.

Eleanor's smile became knowing. "Not at all," she denied cheerfully as she walked to the door to her son's office. "But you were wrong, you know." When CJ just looked at her curiously, she added, "Ty knows the meanings as well as I do."

CJ just sat there with her mouth open staring at the door as it closed. White roses were the symbol of a pure and perfect love. The kind of love she'd always dreamed of finding. There was no way that Ty could have known that. It just wasn't possible. *Was it?* No. He couldn't know. If he did that meant... her heart began to hammer in her chest. *That meant Ty loved her.*

When her boss and his mother emerged from his office a few minutes later, he said, "Cassie, I know this is short notice, but we need to drive up to the Poconos this afternoon. I'm not sure how long it will take so clear my calendar for next week."

"Certainly, Mr. Canfield," she agreed crisply. Liz had accompanied him on trips occasionally and CJ had known that was part of the job when she had taken it. She didn't mind at all. The long drive would give her ample opportunity to find out if he really knew what those blasted roses meant.

"The cabin is rather secluded so dress casually," Ty mentioned as he ushered his mother toward the door. "I'll pick you up in two hours so we can beat the rush hour traffic."

"Yes, Mr. Canfield."

So much for the best-laid plans, CJ thought morosely. From the minute she'd slid into the rear of the limousine, Ty had kept his nose buried in his laptop and completely ignored her. When they stopped for an early dinner and were shown to a table, he pulled out his phone and appeared to be engrossed in it.

He acted as if she wasn't even there and she began to wonder if he had given up on her. The faint hope that his mother might have been right convinced CJ to fight for what she wanted. And she knew just how to do it. The silver eyes flashed as she announced, "I'm going to visit the boutique next door, Mr. Canfield. Could you order for me?"

"Of course," Ty agreed without looking up. As soon as she left the table, he put the phone down and tried to relax. Cassie could read him so well, he was afraid that she would suspect what he was up to if he even looked at her. This was the biggest gamble of his life and it *had* to work.

When she returned and laid a small bag on the table, he glanced at it and asked, "Forget your toothbrush?"

"A nightgown actually," she replied blandly.

His mouth went as dry as ash. The bag didn't look big enough to hold a toothbrush so whatever she had in it wasn't even going to come close to covering that gorgeous body. He almost groaned in agony. "Nightgown?" Ty repeated a bit hoarsely.

CJ had bought the merest wisp of lingerie and told the clerk to put it in the smallest bag she had. If this didn't get his attention, nothing would. "I don't normally wear one, but it wouldn't be at all proper to sleep nude on a business trip," she responded primly. *Ha!* Let him ignore that.

"Good thinking, Cassie," he nodded seriously and tore his gaze away from the bag to stare at the plate the waiter placed before him.

The waiter placed a plate piled high with barbecued ribs in front of her and she smiled in delight that he had remembered they were her favorite. "Thank you for ordering for me... Ty," she said softly.

Not by so much as the flicker of an eyelash did he acknowledge that she'd used his name. "You're welcome," he replied in a tone as bland as the one she normally used.

CJ picked at her food without much of an appetite while he seemed to relish the meal. Frustrated and more than a little angry that her ploy wasn't working, she finally put her fork down and said, "I'm ready when you are."

***

"All right," he agreed and his eyes strayed to that little bag again. Sweet Mother of God, he was dying to see her in whatever it was that fit in that thing. Better yet, he couldn't wait to tear it off of her and make love to her until they both died from pleasure. That thought galvanized him into action and Ty called for the waiter to bring the check.

CHAPTER FIFTEEN

CJ stared at the rustic two-story log cabin perched on the edge of the mountain in awe. "It's beautiful," she said softly.

"It is nice," Ty agreed as he tipped the driver before grabbing their luggage and carrying it onto the porch.

"It's so peaceful here," she said and took a deep breath of the clean fresh air. CJ was a country girl at heart and though she enjoyed the hustle and bustle of life in the big city, nothing could compare with nature's grandeur.

"This is one of my favorite places," Ty admitted as he unlocked the door and took the luggage inside. "I love the mountains."

"So do I," she agreed and followed him in. The ground floor was one large open area with a wall of glass that revealed an impressive view of the mountains. "The view is incredible."

"That's why I bought the place," Ty admitted as he headed up the stairs to the loft.

"It's a wonderful place to entertain clients," she said as she followed him up the stairs. "When are they arriving?"

He placed the luggage on the floor at the top of the stairs and said, "There are no clients."

That brought her up sharply on the landing midway the stairs. "What?"

"There's no one here but us, Cassie," he said softly.

The silvery blue eyes grew huge with realization. They were alone in his cabin and this had nothing to do with business. Ty had brought her here under false pretenses. "You lied to me," she hissed in outrage that he would do such a thing.

"I did not," he denied without a qualm and began walking back down the stairs toward her. "You *assumed* we were meeting clients and I didn't correct you."

"Why?" She asked suspiciously, her heart hammering in her chest. Okay, so maybe she was more than a little thrilled that he had gone to these lengths to get her in his bed because that meant Ty had not given up on her. It did not mean that she had to admit how relieved the knowledge made her or how happy she was with his idea.

"Because this is the closest thing I have to a line shack," he admitted as he stepped back down onto the landing with her.

A frown marred her brow. "A what?" CJ asked in confusion.

He looped his arms around her waist and grinned wickedly, "A line shack," Ty repeated in amusement.

The man had obviously lost his mind because that made no sense at all. "Mr. Canfield..."

"Ty."

"Mr. Can..."

He hauled her flush against him. "Say my name, Cassie."

"Tyrell," she snapped in exasperation.

"It'll do for now," he grinned in amusement before he lifted her into his arms and carried her up the stairs to the loft.

CJ stared around the loft in awe. Every available surface held a vase of white roses and the bed was covered in the delicate petals. "Ty, what..."

"I love you, Cassie," he said softly as he sat her gently on the bed.

"You love me?" She squeaked in surprise, her head spinning as wildly as her heart was pounding.

"I do, and I'm not letting you leave here until you agree to marry me," Ty admitted.

"Marry you?" She exclaimed in astonishment as she stared up at him as if he'd come unhinged. Then the rest of his statement filtered through her dazed brain and she accused, "This is insane. *You're* insane."

He shrugged negligently. "It worked for your father."

"*My*... how the hell do you know about that?" She demanded suspiciously.

"Who do you think gave me the idea?" He grinned devilishly as he toed off his shoes and made quick work of the buttons on his shirt. "By the way, Jake assured me that he'd shoot me if you said no."

"He'd..." her mouth fell open in shock that he had been conspiring behind her back *with her father*. The sight of all that gorgeous muscle he revealed didn't help matters a bit and CJ couldn't even form a coherent thought. "You... he..."

Ty leaned over and placed a tender kiss on her lips. "So, what's it gonna be, Cassie? Are you gonna marry me, or do I spend the whole week seducing you?"

The man was too arrogant by half and this proved it. Oh, she was going to marry him all right, but there was no way in hell that she was going to make this easy for him. CJ folded her arms over her chest and glared at him. "If you think for one minute that I'd marry you..."

"Seduction it is," he readily agreed and silenced her with a kiss.

***

Much later, the two of them lay entwined among the crushed petals and he placed a tender kiss on her forehead. Ty was a man well pleased with his world. He knew that Cassie loved him. She had screamed it over and over again in the heat of passion. Now he just needed to bind her to him permanently. "Marry me, Cassie."

***

She wanted nothing more, but CJ had to be certain that he was completely serious about this. She loved him so much that she'd never survive if he changed his mind. "Ty, are you sure..."

"Positive," he interrupted and tightened his arms around her. "I want you tied to me with so many strings that you'll never get loose. You're a fever in my blood, woman. I can't live without you."

"Do you really love me?" CJ asked with her heart in her eyes and the most beautiful smile on her face.

"More than I'll ever be able to say."

She leaned up on one elbow until their lips were a breath apart and suggested, "Maybe you should show me again."

He shook his head stubbornly. "Not until you agree."

"Ty," CJ pouted as her hand slid down his muscular chest.

"No."

"But, Ty..." she protested as she placed nibbling kisses along his jaw, her hand dipping beneath the sheet that the boner had turned into a tent.

"No, dammit," he groaned when she grasped his overeager appendage.

"Instead of insisting that I marry you, have you considered asking me?" CJ queried devilishly as she trailed her fingernails lightly over his sensitive flesh.

***

God, she looked so beautiful with mischief dancing in those silvery blue eyes and that pale blonde hair falling over his chest. Ty reached up and framed her face with both hands and asked hopefully, "Sweetheart, will you marry me?"

"Certainly, Mr. Canfield," she agreed with a dazzling smile.

EPILOGUE

At the wedding reception, Liz smiled happily at her former boss and said, "I told you CJ was perfect for you."

Noticing the wicked sparkle in her eye, he realized that she had been playing matchmaker. "You did this on purpose?"

"Never doubt it," she said confidently. "After all, I know you better than you know yourself, Ty. CJ really is the perfect woman for you."

"Yeah, but there's one very important detail you overlooked," he pointed out.

"What?" His former assistant frowned in confusion.

"I still need a PA," he complained. Once again Ty was looking for a personal assistant because his was getting married. Since his mother and Cassie's father were moving in with them, his beautiful bride would have her hands full keeping those two out of mischief.

"Oh, I've already found a replacement," Cassie smiled up at her adoring husband as she joined them. "Mrs. Stoutbottom starts Monday."

"Did you say Stout... bottom?" Liz choked on a laugh.

"Mm, hmm," his wife agreed with a straight face and pointed across the room. "I invited her to the wedding so Ty could meet her."

Across the room stood a middle-aged woman in a severe black suit, sensible shoes, tortoiseshell glasses, with her hair in a tight bun. Liz all but collapsed in laughter after taking one look at Ty's look of absolute astonishment. "Sweetheart, tell me you're joking," he choked hopefully.

"Oh, no. She has excellent credentials and I'm certain that she's perfect for the position," Cassie assured him as her lips twitched in amusement. "As long as you don't try giving her fashion advice I think the two of you will get along fine."

Ty stared down at his bride and laughed in delight. Cassie had brought chaos to his well-ordered existence since the day he met her and he wouldn't have it any other way. God, how he loved that crazy woman!

The End

CONTEMPORARY ROMANCE

The Bad Baker Boys Series

Once upon a time in the small town of Lakeside lived a family of handsome men better known as the Bad Baker Boys. Former Navy SEAL Jed Baker raised his sons Matthew, Mark, Luke and John to be badass alpha males. Sparks fly and passions ignite hotter than sultry southern nights when they meet the women who tame them.

Welcome To Lakeside Series

Lakeside is *not* the average small southern town. The residents are unpredictable as hell and romance can be downright deadly. Gossip always runs rampant and is notoriously wrong. Expect plenty of high jinks and ribald humor with unexpected twists and turns. And a goat. On a leash.

ROMANTIC COMEDY

I Boinked The Boss Series

Getting down and dirty with the boss has never been so much fun. These office romances are anything but typical and you'll laugh out loud at the outrageous situations they find themselves in. The path to true love may not be smooth, but it sure is hilarious!

MILITARY ROMANCE

The Invictus Security Series

When the enemy targeted their women, the men of Invictus Security retaliate as only a group of badass former Navy SEALs can. Their mission is the complete annihilation of a secret cabal intent on world domination. They'll rain hell to accomplish it because *failure is not an option.*

REGENCY ROMANCE

The Ashbrook Legacy

You are cordially invited to meet the Ashbrooks, one of the oldest and most revered lineages in England. Despite five hundred years of nobility, the men are notorious rakes and the women are scandalous at best. Take a delightfully wicked romp through Regency London. Historical romance will never be the same!

PARANORMAL

A Howl's Romance

A multi-author series featuring classic romance with a furry twist…

About The Author:

Tonya Brooks is a teller of tales, a dreamer of dreams, and a weaver of words. Her steamy romances contain action, suspense, and humor with unexpected plot twists and turns. You never know what's going to happen next, hence her catchphrase, *It's all smoke and mirrors till… The End.*

She lives in Myrtle Beach, SC with her very own bad boy husband. Most weekends you can find them playing tourist in their hometown, at a festival, or shell hunting on the beach. She's a coffee addict, dark chocolate connoisseur, and lover of all things romance. She loves to read, loathes cooking, has extremely eclectic taste in music, and a wicked sense of humor.

You can connect with Tonya on her web page:
http://www.tonyabrooksauthor.com/
Facebook: https://www.facebook.com/TonyaBrooksauthor
Twitter: https://twitter.com/tbrooksauthor
Email: tonya@tonyabrooksauthor.com
Sign up for her Newsletter: Newsletter Subscribers
Join the Facebook reader group: Tonya's Tribe
Follow her on BookBub for New Releases

If you enjoyed this book, please leave a review at:
Amazon: Amazon.com: Tonya Brooks
Goodreads: https://www.goodreads.com/TonyaBrooks

Made in the USA
Columbia, SC
12 October 2018